THE GODLESS MEN

By

MATT CUTUGNO

Also by Matt Cutugno

THE WINTER BARBEQUE

THE DRACULA LEGEND

STAY THIRSTY PRESS

An Imprint of Stay Thirsty Publishing

A Division of
STAY THIRSTY MEDIA, INC.

staythirsty.com

Matt Cutugno

THE GODLESS MEN

for Chris, Dan, and Lily

The American Civil War brought immense conflict and change to the Kansas-Missouri border. Neighboring States could not have been more different. Post-war, there was semblance of law but yet lawlessness. There were Indians being forced off their land but not without a fight. Outlaws were common, crafty, and well-armed. Indeed there was bloodshed. In abundance too were greedy men who saw the taming of the land as opportunity to amass fortunes. It was the devil's own work.

Book One

Hard Ride and Quick Stop

I

Wasn't hard to kill, least off *he* found it so. That must be what makes men different. Some live by Bible words, others by laws of men. Some raise a family, they work, go to church, one day to the next. For him, it was a question of how to do it, how to get away. He carried a Colt, two knives; he was tall, blond, and strapping. The getting away clean was three things: look sharp, stay calm, and aim straight.

Lessons learned with the Pony Express, though he was not a killer then. Fourteen years old when he started. Lied to get the job, fought to keep it, nearly died doing it. "Skinny, expert, willing to risk death daily," the advertisement for riders read. He rode ponies fast as could be ridden, survived many a close call: the fiercest of Indians, *bandidos*, cursed weather. The boy had a knack. Guess that's why he took to the rebellion so well. Eighteen when the fighting began, he learned to kill straight-off. He waged war for nigh three years, did his duty and more.

He was still at it. Stood in the midday sun, on the 4th of July, in Seneca. He did not abide by windy Kansas, he was from Missoura, so it had to be a powerful reason him being 'round Jayhawks. He leaned against a weather-beaten clapboard shack at an alley that ran to Ledger Street. He was waiting.

Earlier, folks at Redbone were talking about the date, the 4th. Big celebration, it was the birthday of the country. He was there for ale, paid no mind to saloon chatter. The country they spoke of wasn't his, even the allegiance he felt for the other side during the war meant nothing now. Today was simply the day he would start doing what he agreed to do, earn his pay. But at the Redbone, they carried on. A skinny dandy wearing a felt hat with a curled brim brought it up: "I read that back east, New York City, a fine display of fireworks will light the evening sky," he declared.

"Fireworks, what's that, gun shots?" the blond asked.

"Pyrotechnics."

"Pyro what?"

"Pyrotechnics, surely you have heard of that."

"Surely I have not," he replied and stared. He didn't like anybody saying surely to him.

Man got the message. "Good sir, pyrotechnics, fireworks, are small, controlled explosions, colored lights, for entertainment of the masses celebrating, for example, the New Year of 1868."

"That right?"

"Today is the 4th of July, the anniversary of the founding of this country."

"You mean Kansas?"

The man's face twisted, confused. "Our country, the United States of America."

"Where you from, Mister?"

"Originally, Pennsylvania."

"Yankee."

"Just happened to be born there, Kansan through and through I am."

"Ain't you heard? Jayhawks *are* Yankees."

"Sir, Jayhawks were guerrillas. Kansans are not. That would be the difference right there, as I understand it."

"You understand nuthin."

"Perhaps not, I'm not a political man."

The blond took a sip of ale. He grunted "fireworks."

"Very big back east."

Yankee Dandy was talking too much, annoying the daylights out of creation. "Son, get it in your head we ain't back east."

"Good point you raise."

"*Are* we Mr. Patriot?"

"Surely we are not back east." The man said "surely" again. He was stammering like a schoolboy, one drinking whiskey. 4ᵗʰ of July, glory be. Blond finished his drink, nodded at the nervous, fat barkeep who was standing off to the side, and left Redbone. He was thinking he should've shot the fool from Pennsylvania. He had the inclination. But he couldn't very well put a bullet in everyone who vexed him.

*   *   *

Now out on Ledger, he held a hand up over his eyes. The wind was whipping sand. He squinted up the street. There was a gent making his way from a distance, striding with a purpose forced by the brown gale. The blond looked hard at the fellow, it was who he was waiting for. Average of height, overweight, moving in steps that seemed side-to-side, though if that was true he wouldn't be coming forward. The gent huffed and puffed. He held one hand on his hat lest it blow clean away.

Thirty feet between them now, plenty enough for the Colt. The gunman leaned from his waiting spot, took a step into the street. Wind kicked up further, obscuring the sun, making the air thick. Damnedest day. He tracked, no reason to hesitate. He aimed, fired. The weather was so fierce he did not hear the blast though it was him who shot. Twenty-five feet, clean as you please, the unsuspecting gent never knew what hit him. Thud of impact did not send him back right off, the wind held him up. Blood appeared on his vest where the top button was affixed. Some shot.

Seconds after being hit the man was bent over, knees buckling. He dropped hard. Hat fell off, blew down the deserted street. Fellow must have been moaning, but it couldn't be heard.

There was but one doctor in Seneca and he was presently in Hays, a day's ride north. The shot man was doomed to bleed into the next life. The blond holstered his pistol. He turned to the alley where his mount waited. Felt a momentary chill when he had one last gander. Not fair to shoot a man like that but the coward had it coming.

*   *   *

3

Rode a good five mile, looking back now and again. He wasn't being followed, didn't expect to be, he was riding alone. His horse was Boy and the rider now patted its neck. "Boy" wasn't much of a name but few called their mounts anything. He and Boy been together since the war ended, three years. He preferred the company of this horse to that of most men.

Now as night came, he slowed the animal's gait; guided it off the road to a creek's shallows and dismounted. Boy took a good drink. The blond fancied being out under stars, he was partial to a cloudless evening sky. Even during the war, he'd just as soon sleep outside by himself. He cottoned to three things: making money, making women, and being left alone.

Night sky was a sight, had to be a thousand points of light. He lay on his back, head rested against the horse's saddle. He respected the dark, some truth about it. He stared up into the array of stars, quite a show. Just then was a streaking light. In a distant blaze it crossed the sky and descended to the horizon. Folks say shooting stars mean something: birth of a child, great good or bad fortune, some such momentous event. Far as he knew, shooting stars meant nuthin.

*   *   *

They called him Davey when he was riding Pony Express. That appellation he did not take to. Name was David McClure, like the great King David in the Bible. His father was Davey; the man was a surly, hunched backed, no-account who was partial to smacking his wife and child. So when the kid was riding mail for a dollar, he'd threaten anyone who called him Davey. Problem was other riders were older, bigger, meaner, and always ready for a fight. As a youngster, the boy lost many a scuffle. That was nigh a decade past. He didn't lose now, not fist fights nor shootouts.

He leaned up on an elbow from the saddle-rest and reached at the fire, removing a piece of smoking rabbit meat. Waved it in the cool air; took a bite. Tasted passable, though he was not adept at cooking game.

In the morning, he'd head east to Missoura. St. Joseph was the town. Pony Express runs started there April 1860, that was his base. Slept in a sagging bed, a hotel with no name. First time he had a woman, he was nigh a boy, it happened in St Joe. Killed a man who drew on him, it was there.

He was tired. Sleep coming, he contemplated the war. Three years ago now since the end, long time remembering. As he lay on his back surrounded by stars, he thought back to the Hornet's Nest. Federals were set in nice along Sunken Road, midst cedars and outcroppings of rock. Damn, there weren't so many of them, but they were real well hid. Confederates were across the way deployed for battle, with barren fields and fruit orchards between them and the yanks.

The Grays attacked, David and his boys in the thick of it. He was young, full of vim, spoiling for a fight. Fellow to his side got hit, leg broke by a Minie ball; man yelled out and collapsed. Another Gray-coat got hit in the head, spraying blood and brain, ghastly sight that.

The Confederate response was fire from dozens of guns popping into the thicket where the blues were. Lead buzzing into trees, it was startling noise never heard before, like a storm of hornets from hell.

He got tired of running, stopped, knelt in tall grass. His rifle was a Wesson Repeater, a fine carbine. He steadied it against his shoulder. Quiet, he took a breath. Feds were aiming at moving targets, he was not one. He looked for a puff of smoke. Come on Yank, show me where you are. There, he squeezed. Pop of the Wesson, then a thud into the tree line where the smoke came from. David heard the moan, he'd hit a blue.

The boys kept charging, brave and foolish, getting hit this way and that like red rag dolls. David spotted a Yank creeping forward, he fired and hit the man in the neck, least that's where both hands went. Next time he fired, his shot cracked an oak, sending trees limbs and afeared blues reeling.

The buzzing noise, yelling and blood had a morning sun dancing on top. Gray officer gave a whistling order and what was left of the once charging group headed back where they came. They'd done some damage to the Union line, but they got worse than they gave, good buys got kilt. That was the first run at the Hornet's Nest, Shiloh, spring of sixty-three.

Battle of Shiloh got 'im his nickname. Old-timer in camp coined it, called out to McClure "Hey, Quick Stop," and shook his hand. Those tented about understood it meant that the man with the Wesson was a shooter, could stop a soldier dead in his tracks. Quick. The blond wasn't much for nicknames, but he liked that one well enough. The boys slapped him on the back and laughed it up. That's war, the living celebrate they ain't dead.

He woke up from the dream and peed, then bedded back down. Another dream, this one about a mount he had in the Express, a tall, bony, palomino that could run all day. Now rider and mount were galloping, his leather vest flapping in the cool wind. Mail satchel secure; the Missouri River snaked with the road. An easy, safe ride in fine weather, and he was young to boot.

David woke. Shook his head clear, took a drink. He recalled that the palomino in his dream wound up dying with another rider during a run gone-bad in Colorado. Freak snowstorm done it. Too bad, the horse was one good animal.

*   *   *

Two days' ride later, David opened a creaking door. The room faced the street; outside was St. Joseph, Missouri. A busy place, flurry of buckboards, horse riders and those on foot, going about each their business, dogs barking at it all. He wasn't much for the clamor of towns.

In the room two men were waiting on him. One sitting at a fine oak table drawing on a cigar. He was a round-faced big fellow with thick, brown hair slicked back. Standing off to the side was a dark and lean man, dressed in a suit made him look like an undertaker. David sized it up: cigar man was the boss, the other his capable gun.

The former smiled paternally, like he knew the blond, though they had not been introduced. "Cowboy, come on in. Have a seat."

"Fine standing," David replied.

"Suit yourself."

McClure slapped his *chaparajos*, sending sand to the floor.

"Hard ride, eh?" the man with the cigar asked.

"Long ride, wasn't hard."

"I suppose, cowboy, you're used to the open range."

"Second time you called me cowboy."

The seated man made a face, exchanging glances with the other at his side. The boss waved at the air.

"Thought you was one," he said.

"I ain't."

Boss was genial enough. "Was told a cowboy was coming, I can see now you ain't. I'm just making small talk, mister."

David blinked. It was like he didn't speak the language. He thought about Boy tethered outside, wished he was talking to *it*. "I don't make small talk," he said, "don't know what it is."

"Then, let's not do it. You do know who I am."

"You're the fellow who pays me."

"I pay the fellow who does the job." With that the man pulled at the drawer of the desk. He had to move his belly to get it open. McClure placed his hand at the leather of his belt, where a Bowie knife was tucked. Just take a second to have it thrown if anything unexpected came out of the drawer. Man removed an ivory-colored envelope and tossed it on the desktop.

"Here you are, son. Yankee greenbacks as promised, half now, half later. Okay, if I call you son?"

The blond took a step closer and grabbed the envelope. "You ain't my father." David took a gander inside. Cash money. He put it in his coat pocket, patted. "How you know I got the job done?"

The big man drew on his stogie. He might have made fun of McClure, but there was something about the boy with dusty chaps. This was nobody to laugh unduly in the presence of.

"Telegraph," Boss replied. "Heard yesterday that a poor fellow in Seneca got himself shot. Man was a town elder."

"Elder, what's that, a lawman?"

"Heavens no, he was a corrupt no-account."

The blond was unconvinced. "Posse must be out, regardless."

"Must be, though no one knows exactly *what* happened to the deceased, nary a clue." Boss man and his hired gun shared a nod. David got an urge, would like to have shot 'em both right then.

"I was fortunate, bad weather in town that day, nobody out," McClure said as a way of ending the conversation. He ran a hand through his hair. "Where can a fellow get a bath and shave?"

"Outside, across the street, two doors down. Find a man named Procter, he'll set you right up; take care of your horse too." Without another word, the blond turned his back to leave.

"Uh, son, what about the others?" David looked at him, didn't say anything, so Boss clarified: "Those precious others."

As he opened the door, the blond considered in turn the two men. He'd about had enough chatter. "My word is good, and you have it," he declared and departed.

Those in the room waited, listening, until boot steps faded down the hall. Man in the black suit moved to the oak desk. He had a low, rumbling voice and an ominous feeling. "That boy is trouble."

Boss imitated McClure: "You ain't my father!" The men shared a coarse and nervous laugh they'd stifled in the presence of the young buck.

*   *   *

McClure rolled off the woman and onto his back. Took a breath and gazed at the ceiling, mind and body expended. She commenced staring, he wasn't paying any mind. She had red hair and lively eyes, fair features and ample breasts, a small-hipped girl who smelled fine. She moaned as he rode her, he figured she acted excited with all her men, part of the job. Now she stared. Enough to make a man uncomfortable. Not this man though.

"You're good," she said and sighed. He could tell she meant it.

"Am I?"

"Yes sir, indeed." She was younger than him, which made her young to be an experienced whore, which she seemed to be. He leaned up on an elbow.

"Price still the same?"

"What do you mean?"

"Trail hand come in here, you have to take it. I took a bath, I was good, I should pay less."

She batted her eyes, not sure if he was serious. "House rules," she said. He made a sound as close to a laugh as he could manage. He got out of bed and crossed to the open window.

She sat up. "You should put clothes on," she stated.

"You worried about folks down in the alley seeing a naked man in a whorehouse window?"

"No, the wind coming in, cool today, there's been a croup going around."

That's the damnedest thing, he thought. Either she's making a joke he don't get or she's concerned about his health. He didn't have time to consider it more than in passing. "Your face is red," he said.

"I got sensitive skin."

He was not sure what sensitive skin was. Maybe the conversation was the small talk Boss spoke of. Regardless, he put on his pants and boots. Reaching inside a pocket, he tossed a coin. She caught it with two hands.

"Good catch," he acknowledged.

"I meant it when I said you was good," she giggled.

"You meant it," he repeated. He didn't know what this gal was trying to get at. Something made him stop and think kindly.

9

He turned to her before he left the room; she was naked in bed. She looked at him like he had done something for her instead of the other way around.

"You was good too," he said, "next time I'll ask for the redhead."

*　　*　　*

Downstairs there were two rooms off the lobby; one of them was a grooming parlor. He went inside. There was a bushy-headed man holding a razor, standing next to an empty, leaned-back chair, and two other locals sitting smoking. The barber waved his razor at McClure.

"Greetings cowboy, how about a shave?"

"Name ain't cowboy."

"Sorry, what is it?"

"He who wants a shave."

"So be it, have a seat, if you please." David sat down in the leaned-backed seat which the man adjusted. Barber took a hot towel from a heated pot. He was real careful as he applied it to the young man's face. Meantime, the two seated gents were in conversation, paying no one else no-never-mind.

The barber removed the hot towel and then he smoothed a layer of lather on David's face, nice and even. He took the razor to his leather strap, ran it up and down, slow and sure. The blond took a deep breath though relaxing did not come natural. He allowed himself to close his eyes while the barber plied his trade.

One of the smoking gents said something that caught his ear. "They say the man shot in Seneca was President of the Central Kansas Railroad."

"Ain't so," the other said. "He was former Senator from Kentuck."

"He was, years ago, then he joined the railroad."

"I see, was big, regardless, it remains to know who did the deed. Occurred to me it was a Confederate, settling a score."

"There's no Confederates thereabouts."

10

"Then redskins did it, they hate railroads, deceased was a rails man."

The first man spoke in lower tones. "I heard tell the dearly departed had a falling out with the iron horse crowd and was considered disloyal."

David felt the cool, sharp razor run in short strokes along his face. Weird these laggards in a barbershop knew more than he did.

*   *   *

End of day he was alone, top floor of the hotel. Paid a dollar for the room, had a bed of squeaky springs and scurrying bugs. There was a washbasin in the corner and a chamber pot bedside. Sitting in a rickety chair, he had a bottle of whiskey and he pulled on it. He was clean shaved; he'd had a bath, a meal, and a woman. That and getting paid was what St. Joe could offer this time around.

Warm in the room, whiskey was making his head spin. He kept on drinking, got calm and clear thinking. A fat envelope of greenbacks lay on the nightstand and his Colt next to that. It was more money than he had ever had or seen in this world. McClure considered the task he'd undertaken, such thoughts were best not pondered.

Seated at the window in a whiskey daze, he thought again about the Nest. General Beauregard said he had to have that stretch of road. David and his boys did not understand why nor did their officers.

Second charge was soon after the first. The field was still wet with morning dew, Grays were slipping, failing to find footing to shoot good. He had a friend Clem shot and killed in that charge, took a Minie to the teeth and bled to death before the sun was up. The Rebs didn't get more than half way to the Sunken Road on that attempt. They did manage to kill any Blues foolish enough to stand in plain sight or venture into the field in a counter attack.

Third charge was at noon. David had the sense to find a shooting place among rocks two hundred feet from the road. He

11

got settled in with his Wesson. He killed at least three Yanks from there, he was joined by other sharpshooters, and they did damage to the left of the blue position before they heard the call to retreat.

Quick Stop's Missouri bunch got reinforced by stragglers from Mississippi and South Carolina, and took the Sunken Road with a charge mid-afternoon, when the Yanks just plain ran out of alive men. Attack over, David stood among the dead, on the rutted squiggle of a lane running south to Pitts Landing. There you go General Beauregard, you got your road. The boys were whooping it up. The wide field was covered with bodies, like the road was. The field was Gray, the road was Blue, and both were red. There was a peach orchard, it was April, and trees were in flowering bloom. Courtland County boys who fought over there were saying the dead were blanketed in peach blossoms.

Next day, to the surprise of all, the order came to leave. Beauregard had decided a retreat to Corinth, Mississippi was for the best. Two days fighting for nothing. David had killed men, figured now he should've let them live. This way Yanks could let Clem live, or that fellow Short who all the boys liked on account of his harp playing at the fireside. Dumb to charge a position hell bent, kill the defenders, then retreat. That was the first taste of war, David had three more years coming.

Now alone in his room, he reached for the whiskey bottle, empty. He got in bed. Sleep; work to do in the morning.

*   *   *

The smallest part of an orange sun showed east at the flat horizon. He and Boy, in a spanking trot, headed north out of town. The morning air was cold and crisp, the horse snorted clouds of exhalation. The road forked. David led his mount to a branch of the Platte River. Real quiet there, nary a bird call, with thicket running out from the bank, and tall, spreading ash trees along the water. Noisiest thing to be heard was the buzzing of bugs.

Fork was seasonally well traveled. It led to Nebraska and the largest part of the river. Stagecoaches out of Missouri used it; David had trailed one on his way out. Wouldn't be another such conveyance coming around the bend until the same time two days hence. He dismounted, tethered Boy to a red and green holly bush. He watched the water and the bubbling flow over rock mid-river. He considered the sun rising easy in the sky; listened to birds chatter in branches above. Seemed like the creatures were talking with each other which he figured was nigh impossible.

The spot was suited for what he was there to do. He had a view of the approaching trail and could see in advance dust in the air from riders. He knew Boy wouldn't give him away, as the horse was of mild temperament and content chewing on grass and stems.

He found himself pondering the Pony Express. There he was, young and scrawny, riding bareback for shorts runs on some mounts, bare-footed too. He rode eighty miles a time; with a fresh horse every ten miles. Rode daily from April of '60, to October of '61. That was the entire life of the famed Express. He was proud of the job he'd done, never losing a satchel, never backing away from trouble, Indian or other kind. He might have been happy then, couldn't rightly remember now if that was the case.

Reverie got broke by a gust of wind that cleared his thoughts. Foolish dwelling on the past, days that didn't matter, done and gone. So he was thankful the wind made his mind stop.

Cloud of sand and faint sounds caught his attention. David tossed aside a sprig of mint he'd been chewing on, fetched Boy and eased up on top of the animal and gave a slight kick. He stayed low on the horse; he could hear it breathing and its heart beating. He guided Boy into thicket.

Now he saw a man up the road. The gent was alone, riding a sorrel. He was small, wore an ill-fitted cowboy hat; he bounced up and down like an inexperienced rider. David knew right off this fellow was the one he was waiting for, so he stayed hidden but sat up on Boy for a look.

The rider passed, clumping easy as you please, unaware that he was being tracked. David waited until he was well past before he eased Boy back onto the road and followed. It was a quarter mile later the man made it to the river. He was crossing the shallows when he first sensed his shadow. McClure gave his mount a kick and entered the water, closing in a hurry the distance between the two. The muscular sorrel reacted; snorting and pulling its head up. The rider looked back. He called out, "Why, Sir, are you following me?"

David gave Boy one last prod and drew alongside the other horse. Then he jumped off his mount and at the surprised fellow in the big cowboy hat. The force pulled him and his hat off the animal and into the cold water. The smaller man was armed, everybody in Missouri was armed. Too late for that. The blond was heavier, stronger, knew what he was doing. The man he'd taken down was underwater in the river before he knew what happened. David took a deep breath, his adversary did not. Both were under the flow, and even in the shallows of the crossing, it was deep enough. David pushed hard, held tight as they struggled. It was over after an amount of thrashing. The man went limp, McClure kept him under to make certain, then let go. The body surfaced and the current carried it away from the shallows into deeper water. Meanwhile, Boy was jumping nervously. That horse never did like water much, more so without a rider. David grabbed its reins, leading it back to the dry field. He tethered Boy and then cast his eyes downstream. The body was bobbing on the river, heading into town the hard way.

The blond reached into his wet pocket, took a wad of well-wrapped chew. He moved under an ash tree and took off his soaked clothes and wrung 'em. The day was heating up; the clothes would dry soon enough hung along prairie bush. Then he took a chew, a modest wad, he wasn't much for chewing. He was naked as the day he was born. He sat on matted grass, watched the river. He'd killed a man, drowned him. Not sure why he didn't shoot, except the man who paid said to do it this way. Said it'd be better if the deed seemed an accident. What damn fool would drown himself in the freezing Platte by accident?

THE GODLESS MEN

Who was the rider? Older than David, maybe forty. Did he deserve his untimely end? The blond had learned long ago, what you deserve don't matter. He got up, shook his bare body some, let go with a good spit upon a boulder. Across the creek, Boy was feeding on herbage.

II

Some spoke well of Lawrence, Kansas, some did not. Depended on who was espousing. True that the weather was spotty. Winters are cold and windy, summers hot and windy. Climate, though, was the least of it.

One man might note with pride that it was a town founded by high minded who believed in equality, color and creed notwithstanding. Another man would testify how even before the war, bushwhackers from Lawrence went on down the short distance to Missoura burning houses and killing livestock. Divers folk believed they were righteous and what you believed be damned.

The community still smarted from Quantrill's nefarious raid midst the war. Many had loved ones dead from that dark day. Upwards to two hundred citizens were murdered in the streets and fields. Smell of smoke stayed with the town nigh a year, hung in the air like ghosts. Now five years later with war done, Lawrence was reborn.

There were things to recommend. There was the flow of the nearby Kansas River. Because of its location, the town was a natural point to connect with Topeka to the northwest, but more importantly east to Kansas City, St. Louis, and points beyond.

Then there was the postwar arrival of serious railroad money. That meant unbridled growth. The center of Lawrence was bustling as could be, had more saloons than you could visit in a day and not fall down drunk by noon. There were half as many bordellos as banks, which was saying something considering the financiers from St. Louie wearing twenty dollars suits and flipping silver coins at boys who fetched their bags. Opportunity galore awaited smart men.

Thus we speak of two Lawrence, Kansas. One had bled in a massacre. Downtrodden was that place, and dark memories lingered. Second Lawrence unfolded in the present. The future was bright and the grand prize was gold and cash money.

*   *   *

Thomas Powell called it home. This young man had been born down Wichita way, a week's ride south on horseback. Though a reluctant citizen, he was also willing. He had a job to do, he was Lawrence's sheriff. Not a bad occupation, not likely deadly dangerous. Outside city limits the Federal Marshal, named Connor Quinn, had jurisdiction and the man ran a tight ship and had a passel of deputies backing him up. Far as Lawrence went, there were brawlers, thieves, and drunks but there hadn't been serious gunfire in a good spell.

Thom was a tall, trim, clean-shaven man with broad shoulders. His black hair was thick, growing this way and that, and his blue eyes were the color of a summer sky. His imposing appearance was mitigated by a humble way. Sheriff was a most capable man with nothing to prove and it showed.

He carried a Spiller & Burr, fine handgun. Right now, he held the pistol upside down, using the handle to bang tacks into the latest Wanted Men posters that he dutifully hung outside his office on Main Street. The posters were shabby. They came from the state capital in Topeka, and the drawings were doubtful likenesses of the bandits in question.

Sheriff was staring at the last one affixed, Billy Bog Lang, wanted for cattle rustling and mayhem. The Sheriff had known Billy from the war. He was a short, pickle barrel of a man. The wanted poster made him look fit and formidable. Plus Billy was missing an eye, souvenir of battle. In the poster he had two.

Thomas's work was interrupted when he heard throat-clearing and the shuffle of feet behind him. When he turned and flipped his gun back into his holster, he saw Amos Maplewood. Amos ran the west-most saloon in town on Massachusetts Street, a place called "Belongs to Me."

"Afternoon Sheriff."

"Amos."

17

"Latest posters, I see."

"Bunch of *desperados.*"

"I'll keep a sharp eye in the saloon."

"Thank you, that's a good idea."

"I will indeed."

"Bandits are generally drinkers."

"True, though I don't believe it's drinking that makes them break the law."

"Reckon not."

"Some men are born bad."

"Can I help you with something?"

"Wondering if you could stop by my place later, oh around eight, I can offer you ale and hospitality."

"I see, any reason in particular?"

"There's a cattle drive on its way east, today's pay day, this evening the boys will be coming to town."

"Come pay day, herders let off steam."

"I'm afeared of over-much steam. These boys are former Rebs."

"I could have Red or Slim stop by."

"Sheriff, if your deputies want to come with you fine, but everybody knows who you are and if you appear in the flesh, the cowboys will take heed."

Thom was nothing if not polite. "I'll stop by," he said. The barkeep shook the sheriff's hand hardily and then he stepped into the dusty street and left.

Powell did have a reputation, one he was rightly enough proud of. This man was teenaged at the start of the War Between the States. He served the Union bravely, was promoted thrice by its end. He fought in skirmishes and in major battles. Folks told the story that it was Captain Powell who killed William Quantrill in a famous shoot-out near war's end. Thomas was there for that Confederate's last fight, though he never took credit for the bullet that sent the despicable raider into the next life. Regardless,

Lawrence was a Union town, and the man who killed the man who massacred townsfolk was their hero.

*   *   *

That was the public persona. Thing was Thomas was not contented by a long shot. A man wants more than war stories, a reputation, and a job to call his. Firstly, he was troubled by the disturbing times he lived in. Railroads were crisscrossing the land and they needed space. Settlers cleared trees by the forest-full, they needed space. When he was a boy, there were Indians and buffalo in Kansas, it was a good simple life, him and his Mom, and he grew up loving the wild, open land. Then the railroads came, then war came. Now the land was being tamed by the day, and it brought bad with the good. For every God fearing settler who came to the prairie in desire of a better life for him and his family, there was an outlaw or opportunist in a mad dash to money.

What weighed heaviest on Thomas was living his life alone. He was a man without a woman. He never knew his father; his mother was a kind, strong figure who died before the war. While he imagined that one day he would find a gal and settle down, he had not yet done so, and had no idea how to go about it.

One thing certain: dwelling on his state was giving him a pain between his eyes. Good time to amble to the other side of town, clear his mind. His deputies should have already made their rounds, but a second look wouldn't hurt.

Sheriff left his abode, strode past the general store, the Minerva Hotel, the undertaker's, and Tyrel Corral. The noon stage rolled past and into town, he gave a wave to the man who was riding escort. Moustached fellow was holding a yellow-boy rifle and saluted back.

Thom crossed Main to Garden Street. He could see the Federal Bank from that vantage. A few folks were out in the bright sun, crossing this way and that, minding their business. Everything was normal except for the presence of one fellow. He was a short, wiry type who stood near the bank door. He was

19

alone, his quarter horse tied nearby. The man was rolling a cigarette; tipping his hat to ladies who passed, giving a toothy grin. Sheriff did not recognize him nor did he cotton to pretend friendliness. The fellow lit his smoke, walked close to the bank's front portal. When it opened for a patron to walk out, he snuck a look inside. Then he sat on a stoop and smoked.

The sheriff went back to his office. When he entered, Red was comfortably seated at a small table, his booted feet on top. He bolted up with Thom's arrival.

"Afternoon Sheriff."

"Red." The deputy was of average height and weight, carried a Colt Walker pistol in his holster. He was near bald, with a bit of red hair on the sides, hence his name.

"Quiet day in Lawrence," he pronounced.

"Make your rounds?"

"Just got back when you arrived, just now sat down."

"Notice anything at the Federal Bank?"

"Front door has a red, white, and blue bunting."

"Other than that."

"Nothing out of the ordinary."

"I want you to go there now. Find a skinny fellow out in front. He's wearing a wide brim hat. Get a good look, keep an eye out for him another day." The deputy, confused but unquestioning, was happy to have something to do. He placed a hat on his shiny head and left the office.

Thomas allowed that the sneaky type at the bank might just be a farmhand waiting on his boss. But men with badges are well advised to take no chances and err on the side of caution.

*   *   *

Powell had dinner that night at the Minerva, beefsteak with potato and onion, a good repast. By the time he was done with the meal and coffee, it was eight o'clock. He wasn't partial going to a saloon bearing-witness to hollering cowboys. He conceded it was his duty. He met up with Slim and brought him along. Slim was his second deputy, a man who was bushy haired, short and wide, making his name what they call ironic. The deputy might not cast a long shadow, but Slim was a crack shot with a Sharps rifle, a breach-loading weapon that he could aim and shoot fast and true.

Music played as they entered Maplewood's place. Off in one corner were a fiddler and an accordionist on either side of a piano player. They were playing "Johnny Comes Marching Home." War songs weren't popular anymore, folks were dead tired of war, but this one had 'em dancing. Lawrence was Union, but seeing as these boys had served the South, that night it was Rebel music.

Crowd took notice when the lawmen entered. They sat at a table opposite the musicians, their badges plain to see. Sheriff folded his arms on his chest, Slim cradled his Sharps. The barkeep saw the two enter. He tossed a bar rag aside and came over. "Gentlemen, a pleasant evening to you!" Amos announced. He placed two glasses of beer on the table, gave a wink, and headed back.

Meanwhile trail hands and drovers were jumping to the tune. Even the piano player, having cast a stool aside, was dancing as he played. Cowboys busied themselves groping gals. Back in the kitchen they were serving fried potatoes for a penny a piece, a good deal. All and all it was a lively party.

It was then Thomas saw her. A young woman strode up to the bar carrying a wooden tray of empty glasses. She wore a smock over a long blue dress and had her black hair braided in pigtails. Lifting the full tray onto the bar, she then stood with her hands at her sides while Amos removed the glasses. She took a moment to brush strands of hair away from her eyes. She stood like a statue as Amos finished, then she picked up the tray and went to fetch more empties.

She was a female Chinese. No one besides Thom paid her mind. He had never seen one before in person. It was plain she wasn't a party-girl, rather a barmaid. But Chinese? Who was she? How did she come to Lawrence? The woman had a way like she was part of things and distant from them at the same time. She

21

was small framed and slim. Her skin was a medium shade of yellow and clear as a stream. She had lively eyes but kept her glance down, like being noticed was a dreaded thing.

A cowboy approached her as she worked. He said howdy miss. He was drunked-up and tipped his hat in fake politeness. He attempted to embrace the girl. She was a quick one and gave him a kick in the shins. He howled and stumbled. Though she was spunky, she did not cut a powerful figure so the kick was far from harmful. His fellow cowhands guffawed. The bully cowboy skulked. The sheriff witnessing the scene allowed himself a smile. Meanwhile, the girl moved to another table, cleared and wiped. She stopped her work to swat at a bug buzzin' 'round. She returned another tray-full to Amos at the bar, she was a strong enough girl.

Thom had seen plenty Chinamen before. They had hooked up with his Kansan division during the war, as cooks, scrubbers and such. Their kind had been in California for generations, since the gold rush days and before. They were not much for speaking good English, so that kept them apart. Nowadays they were laborers building railroads from Kansas to California, Nebraska to Texas, with plenty of work to do. Fact was politicians and business folk welcomed cheap labor like old friends.

But this one young woman. Thomas was passing curious.

He and Slim didn't stay long. The trail boys were a harmless lot. Some were taking girls upstairs, others content at their tables, tapping their feet to music. The lawmen finished their beers, the sheriff threw a nod to the barkeep who saluted, and then they departed.

Outside, the evening was cooling down; a buckboard pulled into the corral across the street, a dog was trailing it, barking.

"That piano player can play," Slim said.

"That he can."

"Fiddle player ain't shabby."

"He played a fine fiddle."

Slim was a dedicated deputy; having no kin he was readily dutiful so he said, "Sheriff, I'll head back to the office. How about you?"

"I'll walk around a bit, make sure everybody's tucked in."

Deputy said "Right as rain," and strode into the dark night.

Thomas stood still; he peered up Main. There was a dry wind blowing the smell of pine needles. He didn't care if the town was tucked in.

*   *   *

There was a gentleman in Lawrence who Thomas respected and admired. He lived at the Minerva. His name was Joseph Hedley, and he was a retired professor from a college back east. He had been an abolitionist from way back and after the war he settled in Lawrence, a welcoming place for the high-minded. He wrote scholarly books and participated in the rebuilding of the town. He was also a friend to Indians, it was said he spoke Pawnee. This last inclination made him unpopular with railroad folk, the Iron Horse crowd. Simple fact was rails and Indians could not coexist. Regardless, Hedley was a man of esteem.

That next morning, Thomas stood at the hotel room's door and gave a knock. When he heard, "Come in, please, it's open," he did and found the man sitting in a chair next to his bed, reading. The professor was taller than average height and slim, with gray hair and beard. He was of fine features, with kind, green eyes that gave an impression of having seen many things.

"Sheriff Powell," he announced. He took off his reading glasses, put down his book. The two shook hands.

"Sorry to interrupt your study."

"Classical Greeks aren't going anywhere." The sheriff sensed that was a joke, but didn't understand it, though he smiled.

"Would you like to have a seat?" Hedley asked.

"I believe I will." Thomas sat in the other chair in the room. In the presence of this older, learned man, he couldn't help but feel younger than he was. "So, professor, how's hotel life?" he asked.

23

"Not bad at all, folks downstairs clean and cook my meals. It's easy enough to care for these smalls rooms."

"I find that to be true, I live at the Porter, as you may know."

"So you know the hotel life."

"I do."

"How do *you* like it?"

"Passable."

Hedley nodded like he understood the problem. "Young man like you needs a wife."

The sheriff felt blood rush into his cheeks. "I'm hoping that will come," he said.

"I'm sure that it will."

There followed a pause, a good breeze passed through the nearby window. White linen curtains raised and waved at the two men.

Sheriff spoke softly. "I'm here to ask a question about the world we live in."

The professor's face got a quizzical look. He knew his guest as a man of action, this question struck him odd. "The world we live in," he repeated.

"I am wondering what you know about China."

"The great country of China?"

"Yes sir."

"I've never been there, but I have read what has been written."

"Where is it, exactly?"

"The other side of the world. You've been to California, haven't you?"

"I have."

"Travel a considerable distance from there across the great sea, the Pacific Ocean, you'd reach China."

"That's why Chinamen came to San Francisco."

24

"Yes, by the gold rush in forty eight many had come, looking for work and opportunity. By the way, you would properly call them Chinese, not Chinamen."

"Chinese."

The professor sensed the young man struggling with feelings and thus words. Hedley was patient, like a teacher. Momentarily, Thom spoke: "There's a young woman in town, she's Chinese."

Hedley could not hide surprise. "Is there? Aren't many outside of California I'd imagine."

"Why is that?"

"Our immigration laws favor Chinese men, they work cheap. However, their society and culture would not expect or I daresay even allow a young woman to travel outside the country."

Thom could not help but smile. "She is one of a kind."

"I can't imagine how she got here, but she's most welcomed."

"Are all Chinese strange?"

Professor allowed a good-natured laugh. It was plain the sheriff was not a disrespectful man.

"Their civilization is ancient, thousands of years old. Hard for Americans to imagine what that means or what other people in the world are like or have been through. Chinese have a long history and a highly developed culture. They have art and literature, they are industrious, built a great wall across their entire land. They are not a demonstrative people thus they seem different to our sensibilities."

That sounded right to Powell, made common sense, the professor was an educated man indeed.

Thomas spoke. "Folks claim they are inferior to the white man."

"That's an ignorant opinion."

"I reckon."

"You strike me as a man who believes all men are created equal."

Thomas thought about what he believed in. "I do believe that," he said.

"I'd venture to say this Chinese Miss is a real lady."

"Not many like her in a saloon."

"Saloon, what would she do there?"

"She cleans and fetches, helping Amos Maplewood."

"Fancy that."

"She's a hard worker I can tell you."

"Scant credit is given to Chinese building railroads throughout the west, wouldn't know it looking at photographs, a lot of white faces. I have a book here somewhere about China, where did I put that?"

The professor crossed to a spindly table with a stack of bound books on it. He was a helpful sort, but fact was Thom was not much for reading and writing. Hard life and then war had interrupted his schooling. He was about to explain to the professor when there were urgent raps on the front door of the room.

"Sheriff Powell, you in there?" Thomas got up and opened the door wide. There stood Slim, out of breath.

"Red told me to fetch you," he stated. "That fellow is back at the Federal Bank and he has company."

Just like that, the conversation between Hedley and Powell was over. "Professor, I thank you." The teacher gave a salute. The lawmen hurried downstairs.

*   *   *

Armed and ready, sheriff and deputies stood at the head of an alley running into Garden Street. From there they could see the man across the way in front of the bank on Main. He had three horses tethered and he was holding a rifle in a free hand. He looked, with big eyes, up and down the street, like Lawrence was a fascinating town. Thomas sized up the situation and turned to his men.

"Boys, let's say that fellow's two friends are in the bank, up to no good. Red, I want you here, Slim, make your way across to where that rain barrel is set. If men come out of that bank carrying bank bags, then they're robbers. Yell out you're the law, tell them to stand fast."

"What if they don't?" Red inquired.

"You've got the cover and they are in the open."

The deputy was not sure what that meant. "Yeah?"

"They'll be in a neat cross fire, likely they won't be wanting a shootout," Thomas opined.

"What about you, Sheriff?" Slim asked.

"I'm going around the back of the bank, just in case. When they come out front, I'll hear you call them out and I'll join you. They will be trapped."

"Alright then," both deputies offered in strained voices. They were running hot, a tad too anxious for the sheriff's liking. Red and Slim were willing but inexperienced fighters. They reminded him of certain union boys during the war who wound up hard pressed.

Thom shook each man's hand and left them. He went into the general store, out the far door to Main, and crossed the street. A narrow alley led him to behind the Federal. Sun was high in the sky, casting long shadows against the backdoor of the bank. The close-quarters of the alley would not be the best place for a gunfight.

From his vantage he could see down the lane to Merrick's coral and stable. Two boys had a mount outside and they were wiping it down. The horse neighed and stomped its front leg. The sight made Thomas recall his year riding ponies. Lord, he was young, thin as a rail, making him a suitable rider. He rode the hardest shift easy and liked it fine. Young and free, from Sacramento to Saint Joseph, seeing the world, least that's how he felt. His dispatcher in California was a jovial man with a long beard named Simon. He gave the youngster a nickname "Hard Ride." When the boy rode into the home stable he would dismount by lifting his right leg up over the horse and pivoting up into the air and onto the ground, fancy like. "Hey, it's Hard Ride," the dispatcher would say and give him a pat on the back.

Thom's reminiscences were momentary. Now he looked down at his gun and realized he didn't have his usual Spiller & Burr six-shooter, but rather was carrying a five shot Paterson Colt, also a favored weapon.

Silence of thoughts was broken by a crack of rifle discharge coming from the front street. That would be Slim's Sharps. Why did he fire? Then came two blasts, flat, tinny sounds. Red's Colt. The response was a scatter of revolver and rifle shots from the robbers. Then there was silence save shuffling of feet and voices.

Thomas was at the wall of the alley. Just as he took steps toward the shadows and the bank's back door, three men burst out. The force of their exit ripped the portal partially off its frame. The sheriff recognized the lookout. He had a real scared face. The others were older, bigger men. They held bank money bags. All three had guns drawn and ready. They spotted Thom not fifteen feet across the way and they saw the badge glint in the sun.

The Sheriff drew his Paterson. "Hold it there boys, drop those guns and hands up," he offered in a strong voice. Even as he spoke, Thomas guessed what the robbers' reply would be. The wiry one, who wasn't holding a bag, cocked and shot at the sheriff, but he was the shaky, nervous type. His aim was low, to the left. It hit, with a clang, a drainpipe behind the lawman. Only good thing about being shot-at is the smoke and noise coming from the source. It focuses the man being shot at. Powell had come under fire too many times to be afeared now. No sooner had the fellow discharged then the sheriff answered with squeezes from his Paterson. Look-out was hit twice smack in the chest. A bloody thud, thud and the man fell back hitting the red brick of the bank's wall. He slid down in slow motion, his visage declaring "I'm dead."

The older men were ready and able, plain to see they were war veterans. The bearded one held a Le Mat, not an especially reliable weapon. He fired quickly, but was running sideways, and his aim was wild. The sheriff moved a step into the doorframe of the building to his back. He had three rounds left in his Paterson, and here he was shooting into shadows at moving targets.

The second man, who had a wild head of crimson hair, stopped dead in his tracks, tossing money bags that landed in the dust with a jingle of coins. He gripped a Colt and looked like he could use it.

Thom was prepared to get shot. Sure enough the redhead blasted a volley of fire by striking the hammer of his gun with the palm of his left hand, bam bam bam. While two shots hit on either side of the doorframe and splintered wood, the third got the sheriff's left shoulder. Impact was like a kick from a hateful mule.

Lawman steadied his pain. He took his time replying though he did not have time. He fired twice through the burning in his chest. First shot missed and smashed a window of the bank. But the second, with luck, hit the man square in the head. That dropped him quick.

Thom wheeled to the other. That man had set his feet like a shooter would. The Sheriff was slumped at the doorframe but managed to squeeze the last round from his Paterson. The shot barely missed, grazing the outlaw's hip, bad news. A return round smashed into the woodwork inches from Thom's face, the close call leaving a burn on his cheek.

The sheriff's revolver was empty. Time slowed. The sharp smell of smoky brimstone in the alley sharpened senses. The bearded fellow sure had been in gunfights. Had he recognized the sheriff's revolver as a five shot? Maybe he was cool enough under fire to count. Thomas reached to his gun belt for another bullet. The fellow strode at the lawman pinned in the doorframe. It was as sure a death trap as a man could fear. Thom's shoulder was freely bleeding, his ears ringing from the shooting. The man stopped six feet away. He was ugly, had crooked teeth. He threw down his Le Mat, as if to admit it wasn't worth a damn. He drew a handgun, a fine Walker.

Thom was not religious, and even now, as he may have thought the end was nigh, his mind was on the moment. He had a

29

bullet in his hand, was lacking time is all. The robber aimed his black pistol.

Then came a sound, crack, a shot echoed into the alley. Thom recognized the discharge of his deputy's Sharps.

The bearded fellow got hit clean at the base of his neck just right. Real unlucky for him, his head jerked. He dropped the gun like it was too hot to hold and he grabbed his neck with both hands. Red spray shot forth between his clutching fingers and flowed down his chest. The sheriff, who by now had reloaded his Paterson, was ready to fire, but he knew the man was dead and didn't know it yet. Instead, Thom let out a breath and slide to the base of the door. There was a second crack of the Sharps, and the bearded-one got hit in the gut. He looked thunder-struck and fell into the dust like a thick-trunked tree chopped at the base.

Powell could hear voices, yelling. He knew townsfolk would be around presently. Good thing, because the burn in his shoulder was spreading through his body, making blood flow and making his mind spin. The ground came up to the sky and enveloped him. It got real dark.

*　　　*　　　*

When he next opened his eyes, he fancied he was in heaven. He lay in a bed of white linens, in a room with beige walls, there was a smell of medicine. He reckoned he was alive. There was a young woman looking into his face. Try as he might, his vision was blurred and would not focus. It just might be her. It wasn't, couldn't be. There were almond shaped eyes and rosy cheeks.

She held a wet cloth, folded just so. She used it to wipe his forehead, eyes, then entire face. It was a cooling feeling. Her touch was light and sure, her expression attentive. Thomas tried to mouth words. He could barely part his lips. His eyelids were heavy and would not stay open. The room spun and got black again.

*　　　*　　　*

It may have been an hour later or much longer when he awoke. He blinked incredulously at the ceiling. On his back in a bed.

Yeah, he was alive. There was Doc Atley, on the far side of the room. Doc was a good man, lost his wife to Quantrill's massacre, but was always of kind countenance. He was presently drying his hands on a towel like the one in the dream of the woman cooling his burning face. Thomas turned his head. There was a window to Vermont Street below. It was raining and drops pelted the glass with a tap-tap. It was a soothing sound. He took a couple good deep breaths. The doctor, a vigilant man, noticed.

"Sheriff Powell, welcome to the world."

Thom started in to speaking but couldn't. He cleared his throat with a cough and tried again to faint avail. Doc came over with a cup of welcomed water. After a good drink came a low call: "I'm in Lawrence ain't I?"

"You sure as heaven are, on earth and not in heaven." Atley laughed at his own weak joke, he was known for that.

"How long I been out?" Thom inquired.

The good doctor was bedside, he held his patient's hand. "Better part of five days," he began in serious and assuring tones. "Bullet in your shoulder broke into pieces of lead, did not break bone but the bleeding was the thing, we were hard pressed to stanch the flow. Truth is we almost lost you upon sewing you up. Praise God, you are young and strong and that won out."

It was quite a tale and Powell was humbled by it. He did not rightly know what to say. "Much obliged to you, Doc."

The sawbones acted shocked. "Go on, sheriff. I was happy and thankful to do my job after the way you did yours. Three bank robbers down and dead, one who rode with Quantrill himself, you believe that?"

"Was that the tall, bearded fellow?"

"Yes Sir, how did you know?"

"He had a way." Atley didn't know what that meant, and he understood he didn't need to.

Thom spoke up. "Doc, I saw a Chinese woman. Here, in this room."

"You mean Baili."

"Bilee. . .?"

"Her name is Baili. Takes practice saying."

"I saw her in a dream."

"Well, for certain she's real."

"She was employed at Amos's."

"Yes, and it's my understanding good people in Lawrence, among them Professor Hedley, judged that a saloon was no place for a young lady. She's a bright lass for certain, she works here assisting me. Her English improves day by day. It was she changed your bandages and wiped your brow."

"I thought that was an angel."

The doctor allowed a smile. "Of mercy," he said.

Thomas took another drink of proffered water. He never felt as physically weak before in his young life, strange being dependent on others like this. Yet he was thankful for angels.

III

In St. Joseph, Boss man pulled a cigar from his lips to cough a throat-clearing hack. Got a pain between his eyes. He waved smoke away, holding the cigar at bay. Door opened and a man came into the room dressed, as was his wont, in black. He stood and considered his boss.

"You alright, Mr. Whitbread?"

"As rain, Smith."

"Alright then."

"What do we know?"

"Fellow washed up on the shore of County Creek, appears to have drowned. Family coming from Lincoln for the interment."

"Cowboy did his job." Boss tried a smile, instead coughed into a handkerchief. When he took it away, it was blood spattered.

Smith was taken aback. "You should see the doctor," he intoned sincerely.

Whitbread reacted as if he was in the presence of a dumb man. "I am here in the doc's office, what do you suppose I am here for?" was the hard reply.

Smith did not appreciate the words, boss or no. "I'll be getting back to the ranch," he said in a low voice.

Whitbread felt guilty, he responded kindly. "Stick around, say good-day to the medicine man."

"See 'im in church Sunday," Smith said and left.

Boss waited until he could no longer hear footsteps in the hallway and then he coughed hard. Stomach hurt, chest hurt, some bad cold he had. He took a deep breath. Presently, the doctor entered. He was a somewhat corpulent, gray haired man who wore slight, wire-rimmed glasses. Now he gave a smile.

"Chester."

"Doc."

"How's Emily?"

"Emily is fine."

"Her sister and the children?"

"All fine,"

The doctor held a piece of paper in his hand. He waved it. "Got a telegram here from St. Louis, about the test we did for you."

"Some cold I got, like it's on fire down there."

Doctor was solemn. He put the telegram down like dropping a flower on a grave. He was one serious sawbones. The boss didn't like it. He commanded: "Stop fidgeting, your eyes are darting like a weasel's."

"Don't mean to fidget."

"Talk plain to me."

"I've known you twenty years; I know you're a man I can talk plain to."

"Still ain't doing it."

"You have a sickness."

"I know."

"You got a cancer."

"Cancer, what's that?"

"It's a disease."

"Like consumption?"

"Consumption is an infection in the lungs. Cancer is something else."

"I don't understand a word you're saying."

"Would you put that cigar down?"

"Doc, I'm a busy man, it's horse-breaking season, I don't have the time. . ."

"Just be silent and listen!" By the end of the short sentence the doctor's voice was a sharp point. Wasn't like him. Boss pushed the end of his smoke against the bottom of his shoe, putting it out. He tossed the stub into a tin cup set on the windowsill. It got quiet, the air cleared.

Words came in measured cadence: "Cancer is a disease where cells in the body grow uncontrolled, they are destructive, attacking and killing healthy cells, man gets sick fast. You have cancer. In your throat, lungs, stomach, lower intestine."

Chester spit out: "Medicine."

"Can't treat the disease that you have; can only ease the pain."

"Ease the pain," was a faint echo.

"Yes Sir."

"How do you do that?"

"With narcotics."

Boss was flummoxed, like he had heard an incomprehensible language. Doctor moved close and put a hand on his patient's shoulder.

"I'm dying?" Whitbread asked.

"A month."

"A month, what can I do in a month?"

"Chester, you can make peace with your Maker."

Boss blinked at the doctor and got red, fast. He bolted up from his chair like his seat was on fire. "I am not making anything with my Maker. You have made a mistake, or the fools in St. Lou have."

He lunged at the doctor's white coat and grabbed the lapels. Grimacing, he shook his friend, who let him do it. Finally, out of breath, Boss pushed away. He sniffed, visage bright red. Didn't have his handkerchief, so he coughed blood into the palm of his hand, then wiped it on his pants.

*   *   *

David sat in a crevice of rock, atop a hill sloping sharply to the road leading out of Hays, Kansas. A Springfield .58 was leaned nearby. He had his knife and was whittling to pass time. It had taken him better part of three days to ride to Hays, he hadn't talked to another soul, only Boy for company. Camped out nights with a fire for warmth and dried buffalo meat for sustenance. Got to his destination ahead of the game, he welcomed the opportunity to do nothing.

He wasn't keen about what he'd been up to. Killing in war was duty, do it or be killed yourself, made common sense. And he never had no problem killing those who drew a gun bearing him ill will. Bible says eye for an eye in plain language. This time, he did dark work for greenbacks. He wasn't a man to do another's bidding, but he was one who needed greenbacks. He struck a deal to kill men, dastardly types all. Only good thing that could be said he was half finished.

He looked up from his whittling toward the horizon, spotted dust kicked up into the air from someone's approach. It was what he was waiting for. He tossed away the maple branch that was looking like a boat and put his knife into its sheath. He picked up the Springfield.

Intention was to hit a moving target several hundred feet from his position. Not easy, few would try in earnest. He'd learned in the rebellion how to go about it. By now he had a knack. Shoot with the wind, so he placed himself just so among the rocks. Use the gun's sight properly, never sight the target head on. Shooter had to have a feel, like the gun's lead is willed to where it's going. Takes doing to master the task.

Buckboard approached, pulled by two quarter horses. There was a young fella holding the reins, snapping them lightly, nary a care. His passenger was a gray-haired gent dressed in a brown suit. Smoking a corncob pipe, he was looking at the younger one. Perhaps he was saying it was going to be a hot day in eastern Kansas seeing that the sun had burned the early morning cloud cover, leaving a yellow ball of fire in the high sky. Maybe those on the buckboard were talking about that, the weather, small talk.

David had taken his hat off; his hair was a wind-blown tangle. Never did like to wear a hat when he was shooting. It was time. He positioned himself in the crag, legs spread just so, and he got still. Then he raised his .58, commenced tracking the buckboard, and then his aim found the older fellow in a brown suit. Wait, he held his breath, wait, he squeezed.

*   *   *

Marion Harker was Pastor of the Baptist church in St. Joe. He was a good man, tad strange looking though. His body was barrel shaped. Top of his head was bald, he kept it shiny; he wore a moustache with waxed tips. He was broad shouldered and short-legged. He kept a bearing like he had all the time under heaven to get done what he was doing. Fingers were stubby, his hands nearly as wide as they were long. Folks said he had meat hooks at the end of his arms. All in all, the man might have made a comic figure, if he wasn't so respected.

He'd been in Buchanan County for years but was such a private sort that his personal history was the stuff of rumors. It was certain he served the south during the War Between the States, and that he originally came from the Carolinas. Folks testified he was a natural born fighter, Lord in heaven he had fought at Gettysburg, all three days, bloodied but unbowed. Soldier Harker had been awarded war medals. Though he never bragged nor displayed the decorations, he kept the ribboned trove in the cottage behind the church that he shared with his wife. When you heard him on a Sunday from the pulpit, you conceded stories about him because with his booming voice and imposing physical presence, he made the congregation believers in a God who was the dispenser of justice, fair and sure.

Now he was in the back room of his cottage. With his shirtsleeves rolled up to his elbows, he was working on Sunday's sermon. He held firmly a worn but sturdy Bible as he strode the room, speaking in a soft voice of import.

"What can we imagine about the fire of hell? Fierce the flames, searing and perpetual. What will our weak flesh experience? Pain so sure as to make angels weep and make our own pale countenances unrecognizable. Satan has tools, like men do. Men use tools to plow fields, shoe horses, construct homes and towns. The Devil uses them to doom men's souls. Satan's tool is temptation. There are divers kind. Today, I speak to you of Greed."

A knock on the door of the room stopped the reverend as his voice was rising. He took a breath that turned into a sigh.

There was another rap. Exasperated but unfazed, Harker put down the Bible. "Come in!" he commanded.

Chester Whitbread, the Boss, entered with hat in hand. "Reverend," he said simply and said nothing more. The preacher looked at his guest as if he was not expected, which he was not. Boss wobbled as he stood. He held a small black bottle in his hand.

Harker nodded. "Mr. Whitbread," he pronounced.

"Call me Chester," came an earnest reply.

The preacher knew well enough this man who stood there. Whitbread was no joker and so the silly expression on his face was most suspicious.

"Have you been drinking?" was the question.

Chester was offended and acted like it, though he was swaying like a sailor on shore leave. He held the bottle up for inspection.

"This is medicine," he said. "Doctor gave it to me, called it, called it Laubadum."

"You mean Laudanum."

"Laubadum, yes, made from, from. . ."

"Tincture of opium."

"Opium, how did you know?"

"I'm well read. Why are you taking Laudanum?"

"I'm ill." With those words, the boss closed his eyes, stood there and got still. The Reverend was understandably puzzled.

"Mr. Whitbread?"

His eyes opened, he was acting queer. "Ill, that's what they tell me. Cancer, it is." Boss smiled at the preacher, stifled a laugh like a naughty schoolboy. The opium was strong, making him forget he was being consumed inside out. Harker reached out steady and directed Boss to a chair and had him sit.

Pastor's tone was soft. "I'm sorry to hear this terrible news. I want to help, are you here to offer prayer?"

Boss took the deepest breath, shook his head. The man was crestfallen. "As you are aware, I'm not among our most religious folk.

"I do not see you at service regularly."

"I'm not acquainted with the Lord."

"Good Sheppard knows all his charges," came a voice seeking to sooth and assure.

Boss was not assured, he sank deep into the chair. "Emily, my dear Emily. We had the talk, the one at the end of life. She made me realize. Helped me take stock. So now I know there are damnable things I must own up to."

Whitbread stopped speaking. He ran a hand over his head and stared at the carpet like the pattern was fascinating. The preacher stood right there, a drover over a stray. Boss made a sound, its meaning unclear until he began to sob, even as he sunk further into his seat. Strange magic, Whitbread's mood turned, now crying like a baby. Shoulders heaved, tears burst and ran down his fat cheeks. His sobs were like a child's. Here was a ruined and broken man. Harker placed a hand gently on Whitbread's shoulder. It took a spell for the man to calm down some. Harker gave him water, which he sipped.

Boss wiped his eyes with his sleeve, and spoke. "I'm here to clear my conscience. If I'm false now, with the end nigh, the vengeful God will take it out on my family. I have grandchildren, precious things, can't have the vengeful God after them."

"Chester, what have you done to be so afraid?"

"I did sins."

"We all sin."

"Do we all pay a man to kill for us?" Whitbread looked into the preacher's wide face, wet streaks running down his own. Then he cast his eyes to the floor again. The Reverend pulled a chair up, sat and folded his hands over the bible.

"Am I to understand that you have had men killed?" Harker asked.

"I was in straits, dire straits, might lose the ranch, impossible. Thought of it as getting rid of trouble, making a better future for me and mine. Told the boy the men deserved it. He was a believer for cash money."

"What boy?"

Instead of answering, Boss moved his head up and down like a horse, took a sip from the black bottle.

*   *   *

The redhead was on top. She gave his neck small kisses. Girl whispered in his ear: "You take your pleasure whenever you want."

He said nothing. Yes he would do that, he was a customer and she was a whore, why wouldn't he take his pleasure? It was his second time with her, she was the best of the lot. He guessed the silly girl was touched in the head.

When he did finish, she stayed, holding him. She leaned up on his chest.

"Do you love me?" she asked.

Had to be the dumbest question, the blond ofttimes would say something cruel in response to such talk, but he didn't feel like doing that.

"I never loved anybody, darling," he said ruefully.

The redhead reflected on his words then let out a sigh. "That's too bad," she said.

"It is," he echoed.

After a while, the two got out of bed. David sat in his skivvies at a window overlooking the street. He rolled a cigarette. She was standing in front of a mirror, buck naked, pinning up her hair. He watched her, she had a fine body.

"You know something," she said like she was talking to herself though she must have been talking to him, "I never intended to be like this, a whore. My parents died in the war, I was twelve years old, had an aunt take care of me then she died of consumption. I fell into the life. I don't expect to do this forever."

David considered the girl. "You should not," he stated. It was like he was giving advice, which he never did and didn't know how. His words made her smile.

"Do you expect to do what you're doing forever?" she asked him. David was not a talker by a long shot. He did not answer the redhead. But she made him ponder. He blew smoke out the window. Moments passed.

Finally, he spoke: "I do not expect to be doing this forever."

*   *   *

After David had left, she sat robed at her vanity. She wiped a damp cloth over her face, removing make-up. There was a porcelain bowl set with water in it, now she splashed her skin clean, then dried with a towel. An oval mirror on the tabletop allowed her to stare at herself. "Hello there," she said and dabbed fresh powder in case she heard from downstairs about another job. She was hoping no one wanted her. There was something about the last guy, the blond. He was a strange one. He seemed to have heart even if it was dark. She was partial to a dark heart.

There was a knock on her door and she got up from the vanity. There were more knocks, banging. "Hold on, hold on," she said in a rising voice. She fixed her attire and yanked the door wide open.

There stood the sheriff of St. Joseph, a man named Bailey. The whore knew him to be most capable though naturally they had not been properly introduced. A chubby deputy was with him, name of Clyde, who was in fact a not-infrequent customer of the establishment. With the lawmen was none other than Pastor Harker - what in the world was *he* doing here? The preacher considered her like she was scurrying vermin. The distain chilled as damp wind does, the redhead clutched the top of her robe.

Bailey was a tall, dark, middle-aged man. Fit and square-jawed, he acted real professional. He tipped his hat at her. "You alone?" he asked. She looked away from his fierce eyes, handle of the gun hanging at his side glinted in the hall light.

"I am alone, if you come in you will see that I am," she answered strongly.

"We're looking for a fellow."

"Fellows come and go around here," she announced with a glance at Clyde, who got red as a tomato in August.

"This man is blond, a rangy type."

"He was a Rebel, might still be garbed in some gray," Harker added, speaking in a faint voice, like he didn't want to speak at all in a brothel.

"Doesn't sound familiar, I am sorry." She stood there solemn-like. A good actress, the men could not tell if she was being respectful or making fun.

"His name is McClure, and we suspect that he has been a patron of this establishment," Bailey added, even as he judged such details would be lost on this girl.

"They call him Quick Stop," Clyde added, helpful-like.

She laughed politely with a hand at her mouth. "Quick Stop? That does not sound like my last fella. He was not quick and he would not stop."

It was a shocking thing, those words. Reverend let out a sound between a grunt and a gasp, the Sheriff looked as if to apologize for the girl, and Clyde snickered. Bailey took a step into the room and pushed the redhead's face with an open hand. She yelled out as she fell back on her behind.

"That was not necessary," she protested while seated on the floor.

The Sheriff was unapologetic. He stepped into the room and stood over the fallen. "Miss, we are here on a most serious matter. It is life and death, do you understand? You come upon a rangy blond name of McClure, you let me know pronto," he ordered with a pointed finger. After that he offered his hand to the fallen. The redhead reached out and was lifted up from the floor. She brushed at her robe as Baily turned and led the other two down the hall. They were gone.

She brought a hand to her mouth and felt. She had bit her tongue; there was blood on her fingers.

IV

Folks thought well of him before but as news of the bank shootout spread, Thomas Powell was held in highest esteem. He had faced-down and shot-it-out with three despicable robbers, one a former member of Quantrill's irregulars. All three kilt, that's Justice. Citizens in bars drank to his heroics, and reenacted the bloody affair, great fun in the retelling. Kansans are morbid like that.

Slim had a hand in the fight for sure. True a bullet from his Sharps had taken care of the last shooter, it was also true that the man had panicked when the villains emerged from the Federal. The deputies failed to call out stop, and then Slim shot his weapon in haste, his was an itchy trigger finger. Red followed suit. The robbers answered with staccato gun fire. In ensuing mayhem the three scurried back into the bank, through it, and out the alley where they were confronted by the sheriff. No Sir, the glory from that eventful day was Powell's.

He was recovering from his travails, better than could have been expected. Back doing his duty, he was making midday rounds on Main. It was a fine enough day with cumulus clouds in the blue sky obscuring an otherwise bright sun. Store keepers waved as he passed their front windows; folks called out across the street, "Sheriff, good day to you!"

It was when he reached the residential, west end of town that he saw her on the front steps of the rooming house. She was sitting pretty as a picture, holding a parasol up against the sun. Her hair was pinned atop her head, with wisps hanging down either side of her face. He tentatively raised his hand to her in greeting and she waved back tentatively. He swung open the front gate and walked the short distance to the steps. She stood as he arrived and he tipped his hat and removed it.

"Good day, Miss," he said.

"Good day, Sheriff," she replied in soft tones of accented English. She lowered the light umbrella and closed it.

"I never thanked you proper for helping the doc take care of me," Thomas stated earnestly. She could not hold his gaze, though she tried. The image of shyness, she held the parasol with two hands behind her back.

"You are welcome, it is truly my honor to help you and the law." Her words made him smile. "I hope you are feeling better," she added.

"I am, thank you, up and about."

"I don't know up and about, sorry."

"Up and about just means doing your normal things."

"I'm glad you're up and about." Just then wind gusted, smelled of jasmine from the garden.

"We have not been introduced, my name is Thomas Powell." He offered a hand and she considered it, not sure how to proceed. She released her parasol from a two-fisted grip and shook his hand. Her grip was sure.

"Pleased to meet you Thomas, my name is Baili." He listened carefully so he could recall the appellation, to his ear it was a foreign name indeed.

"Pleased to meet you Baili," he intoned and she smiled like he pronounced it okay. He wanted to ask *who are you, what is it like in China, how did you come to Kansas?* Didn't fit the occasion.

"I imagine you live here," he said of the boarding house. It was owned and run by a matron named Mary Dwighton, who lost kinfolk in the raid of sixty-three.

Baili cast her eyes at the two-story cedar-shake dwelling. "I am there," she said, indicating the top floor, "This is the proper place for a single girl like I am." She pronounced the words in a way that suggested they were someone else's.

"Miss Mary is a fine lady," the Sheriff said. Baili smiled and Thom noted she had nice teeth. "I'm sure she'll look after you," he added.

There was silence then. He shifted and the wood floor of the porch creaked. He put his hat back on. "I should be continuing with my rounds," he offered.

"Of course, Sheriff," she nodded.

He started to depart but even as he took a step he felt cowardly and could not abide by that. He stopped and turned back to her. He spoke impetuously, though he was not an impetuous man.

"Baili, would you have dinner with me this evening?" he asked.

She blinked, twice. "Dinner?"

"Something to eat, at the Minerva Hotel." The young woman, who had a natural redness to her skin, got redder still. It took her moments to compose herself.

"I cannot," she said.

"You cannot?"

"I cannot," she said again the same exact way, incredulous.

"Why may I ask?"

"It's not proper."

Perplexed, he inquired, "What is not proper?"

"I am Chinese."

He did not reply straight off. He did not pretend to not understand. Did the Minerva allow non-whites into their dining room except to remove plates? Thom pondered how things were against how things could be. He got steely. "Miss, this is a free town. That means I'm free to ask you and you're free to come with me if you have a mind to."

She seemed to not understand everything he had said. A sinking feeling arrived. Had he made a mistake with his words? Perhaps he was wrong to stop and talk thusly to her, a young woman he barely knew. Then her reply ended doubtfulness.

"I have a mind to," she said.

"Would eight o'clock suit you, Baili?"

"Yes, Thomas," she answered.

He touched the brim of his hat and then he left the front yard of Dwighton's. As he continued his rounds on Massachusetts, he entertained the notion he was fortunate to get shot.

*   *   *

Upon his return to his office, there was a surprise. Half a dozen horses were tethered to posts and men milled about. He saw their badges glistening in the sun. They were deputy marshals from Topeka. That was a long day's ride away, what brought them to Lawrence?

They were a lean lot; dressed in the long, beige riding coats lawmen in these parts were want to wear. One carried a shotgun in his arms reminding him of Slim; another mustached fellow had his coat tucked behind the butts of pearl-handled six-shooters, fancy-like. Their postures declared they thought a lot of themselves. Here were men to handle any scrape.

After he shuffled past them and into his office, he was greeted by Marshal Connor Quinn himself, sitting at his desk like he owned it. Slim was at his side, looking much relieved to see the sheriff. "Captain Powell, good evening," Slim said strangely since he never called him Captain. With that, the marshal got up from the desk and shook Thomas's hand.

"Powell, been a while, how are you?" The Marshal was a giant. He was a dark, thick boned Irishman who seemed smiling all the time, though his appearance was more intimidating than cordial. "Nice work at the bank, three robbers dead as iron rails, that's how we like our robbers," he said and winked.

"What brings you to Lawrence?" Sheriff asked. Quinn cracked his knuckles, then slapped Slim on the back as he moved away from the desk.

"My boys and I were passing through, thought I'd pay a visit. Something has come up the past few days." Marshal grunted, sheriff waited for him to say more but he did not. Finally, Thomas turned to his deputy. "Why don't you wait outside, keep the Marshal's boys company." Slim looked confused, came easy, then he took Thomas's suggestion and clumped out the door.

Quinn produced a thin cigar, bit off the tip, and spit it directly into the spittoon kept on the floor on account of Red's habit. He reached into a vest pocket for a piece of folded-up paper. He flicked it in the air to open it. It had a man's likeness, the word Wanted was printed in big letters.

"Know this here boy?" Quinn asked. The poster was not the best drawing. Still, the sheriff considered the image on the paper.

"Looks passing familiar."

"Does it?" the Marshal asked hopefully.

"Not rightly sure."

"He's tall, blond, and a fighter. Name is David McClure, out of Kirksville, Missoura, name ring a bell?"

Thomas steadied the edge of the paper with three fingers. "Marshal, this fellow looks to be a young gun, lot of those."

"This one rode Pony Express. You rode Pony Express, didn't you?" The Marshal's words surprised and called for a reexamination of the likeness. Thom was barely seventeen in 1860 when he started to ride, and in a year of trips from Sacramento to St. Joseph he met or heard tell of most other carriers. The man in this wanted poster had a stern countenance, no boy, some ten years from being a pony rider.

"Don't know the name David McClure, there was a firebrand back in the day name of Davey, this could be him."

"Did you know him?"

"Our paths crossed, never met him, heard stories of his scrapes, though he was a good rider."

"He was a Rebel, fought in Tennessee, Georgia. Had a war-name, they called him Quick Stop. Idea was his fighting stopped men dead in their tracks."

Sheriff knew about the marshal, about how he did not have a war record. Quinn served neither the Union nor the rebellion, unusual for anyone in those days who fancied himself a fighter. Thomas could not help but say something that danced around that fact: "Just about everyone fought in the war, Marshal."

The Topeka lawman got the slightest red, but stayed cool and stared hard. "Point is this fellow is wanted by the States of

Kansas and Missouri and we expect him to be in Lawrence soon if he is not already here."

"In this town?"

"Yes Sir."

"Doing what?"

"Doing what he does, lawlessness." Quinn blew a cloud of stinking smoke. Thom was suspicious, this was not the whole, entire story.

"What's McClure wanted for?" he inquired.

"Cold blooded murder. This villain shot a man in Seneca, on the 4th of July, then a fellow in Hays, two weeks later. In between a man drowned in the Platte and McClure is the man we are after for that."

"Why did he do those crimes?" Seemed a fair question, kill a man here and a man there made no sense. Quinn just shrugged.

"I'm only a lawman, not the knower of nefarious plans." Thomas waited for more of an answer. When there was none, he spoke.

"Why don't you and your capable deputies track him down? If he is in Lawrence, your authority exceeds my own anyway."

Quinn scratched at his face then he leaned in, secret-like. "The James boys been seen east of Topeka. I will be off after them. Jesse and Frank have kilt more folk than this Kirksville bastard."

He was speaking of the notorious Jesse James Gang, former members of Quantrill's raiders, who were now in the habit of robbing railroads, banks and stagecoaches.

The sheriff picked up the paper likeness of McClure. He was not satisfied with what he was being told, still he had a duty. "My deputies and I will keep an eye out," he assured.

"That's a good man," the Marshal said and gave Thom a slap on the back that was not appreciated.

*   *   *

Face of the fellow at Minerva café got long as a horse's when he saw Sheriff Powell and his dinner companion. His grin was toothy but darting eyes betrayed him. There was a Chinese in his place. She was with a lawman and this was Lawrence, town founded on the living belief in equality. Guess that also meant women from China. Here was a test of those convictions.

"Sheriff, good evening," the nervous one started.

"Good evening to you."

"What can I do for you?"

"We would like to enjoy the hospitality of dinner." The man blinked a couple times and motioned gracious-like to a table. The two made their way. Thomas pulled a chair out for Baili, then eased it back as she sat. He took in the room. He liked seeing Jayhawks squirm. Sure these people were not impolite and did not gawk but they couldn't help but fidget.

"This is a nice place," Baili said like she meant it. They started in talking. Her English was simple, she was smart, and tried hard to speak proper. Turned out she came to these parts with her father, who got a job working the railroad. They had started on in San Francisco, she was young enough to pass for a boy, thus did she accompany him. Sadly, he died from typhoid fever, leaving her on her own. After the war, she made her way to Lawrence, hearing it was a welcoming locale. She said that someday she would return to her homeland, she had aunts and uncles, and that she missed the places of her childhood in a village on a great sea.

Baili no longer looked like a boy, no indeed. Her eyes twinkled as she spoke in a soft voice of strong conviction. Her body was fit, shining black tresses flowed and smelled of flowers. This evening she wore a cotton dress with a white lace shawl over her shoulders and a blue ribbon in her hair.

"I think we make others uncomfortable," she said referring to sneaky stares from the clientele.

"We do and I enjoy it," Thom answered and the two had a giggle. Baili held an open hand over her mouth, lest it would be unseemly.

*   *   *

50

After a fine dinner of trout and fixings, they walked back along Main to the boarding house. It was a cool summer evening, the Kansas sky was lit with stars. This was a new experience. He hadn't known many girls, felt nothing special for the ones he did. Baili was different.

They reached the white picket fence of Miss Mary's. He had a thought, he turned to her. "Do you have religion?" he asked. Odd question, but he had a notion of attending church service with her, that was a thing men and women did together.

"I believe in Buddha," she replied.

Thom did not know who that was. He considered her words. "Is that a holy man?"

She was pleased with his assumption, starlight made her face glow. "Yes, he was a man who lived long ago," she answered.

Thom was not acquainted with religion. Still, he hoped there were such things as holy men. "What did Buddha believe in?" he asked.

She glanced up then down the road, as if their conversation was a secret thing. She kept her eyes cast down, and even in the dark he could she her cheeks redden.

"He believed in the world," she said. Thom made a face like he had an idea what she was talking about, though he did not.

"Do *you* have religion?" Her question caught him off guard, though it was a logical thing to ask. He did not know what to say, so he told the truth.

"I do not. I was never introduced to such things," he answered haltingly. She appeared ready to say something, but she didn't. He seemed a tad uncomfortable, Baili took her cue from that. Instead, she opened the gate of the picket fence and then turned to him. "I much enjoyed dinner and our conversation," she said with certainty. He wasn't sure how to reply, settled on "I truly did too." She considered him with a smile and he returned the favor.

"Good night, Thomas."

"Good night, Baili." She turned and walked with a light tread up the path to the steps and the front door. He waited, would she turn back? She stopped at the portal, gave a wave, went inside.

He stood under the big sky.

*   *   *

Red and Slim were in the sheriff's office on Main. Red sat in a pine chair leaned against the jail bars. He had the usual chew, dark streaks dripping down his mouth. He spit into the spittoon from a good distance, making a sound between a ping and a clang. He let out a laugh at what him and Slim were talking about, his teeth shown brown. Not the prettiest sight in Lawrence that morning. Slim had a long, thin Mexican cigar hanging from his lips but, as was his wont, he was not smoking. He took it from its place, pointed it at Red.

"Let me tell you about those James boys," he began. The two had been talking about Missouri's famous outlaws, the gang of Jesse Woodson James. "Everybody says Jesse is the one, but it is Frank who is the better shot."

"With what, rifle or pistol?" Red inquired.

"Both."

"So why ain't he the leader of the gang?"

"Jesse is plain meaner. Leader is always the one with no conscience."

"Among outlaws."

"That's what I meant."

"I understand that the gang used dynamite on a St. Louie Line Train, blew up women and children, blew them into the sky."

"You read that in a dime store novel."

"They would not print it if it weren't true."

"My friend, you can't read, you just go by the pictures."

"You read good for a Dutchman." They laughed dumb at the chattering talk. Just as Red let one go into the spittoon, ping, the Sheriff entered the office. First thing Powell did was take off his hat and toss it on a hook. He did not like hats much.

"Boys," was all he said. Then he sat in the chair at his desk, the chair squeaked some. Deputies recognized a quiet mood. Red got up from against the jail bars, pulled up his pants some and pointed to the Wanted Poster tacked to the wall nearby.

"Slim and I been looking out for this *desperado* McClure, we was just talking about him." Thomas figured that they had been doing no such thing.

Slim joined in. "I was at the printer's this morning, made copies but the likeness is none too good. In fact, the man there thought it was a likeness of Red, wanted me to arrest him."

The boys guffawed. The sheriff was not one to join in, but he wasn't one to cut it short. Deputies got piddling pay and long hours, if they acted like schoolboys now and again, so be it.

"I don't imagine that outlaw will be coming around Lawrence," Thomas told the two.

Slim acted disappointed. "Paid three cents for them posters."

"Sheriff, you figure McClure skedaddled?" Red asked.

Thom was sanguine, shifted in his seat. "I figure we're putting on a show for Connor Quinn," he said. At the mention of the Marshal, another wad hit the spittoon. While Red was wiping his chin, he noted, "He's a funny sort, that Mr. Quinn."

Slim was quick to echo, "I never met a man knows what that fellow did during the war."

"Marshal did not fight in the war," Thomas answered.

Red had to clear his throat to speak. "Was he an apocary, an apothecarist. . .?"

"He means druggist," Slim offered.

"He was not an apothecary. Neither teacher nor professor. He was one of many who paid cash money for a substitute."

"Three hundred dollars?" Slim was disbelieving.

"Where does a man during war find three hundred dollars," Red added.

"Don't kid yourself, boys, this country is full of rich folk," Powell began. "They like to keep it quiet about how much they have."

It was then the sheriff's eye caught a printed piece of paper on his desk and reached for it. "What's this?" he asked.

Red hit his forehead with the heel of his hand. "Sorry, plumb forgot. That's a telegraph message arrived for you."

"What does it say?" Thomas said as he began to read.

Slim took the cigar out of his mouth and held it in the air. "Red here can't read a lick. I read some, but it was written in a peculiar way. I do know it was from Topeka, and it says to Sheriff Powell. Yes Sir."

It was indeed from the state capital, from Marshal Quinn. The sheriff read the message slow and sure. "Kindly be advised," it began. It went on to reveal just who in Lawrence the outlaw McClure was after. When Thomas read the name, it gave him a start. It was Professor Hedley.

"Red, stay here," he ordered. "Slim, get armed and come with me."

*   *   *

David sat on windblown grass, in idle time, nary a thing to do. Boy was nearby, tethered to a creosote bush. He watched the horse. The animal held its head down and steady, its large eyes unblinking. A fly buzzed, landed on its ear, and stayed there until the ear twitched and the bug flew. It made the blond wonder: do horses think? Do they do anything besides mind the will of their rider and eat and such? He leaned in to look closer at the animal. Boy reared its head and snorted loud and turned away, impatient. Darnedest thing, horses don't like being stared at.

He was a half-day ride or so outside of Lawrence. Had one last business to do to complete that which was expected of him, what he was paid for. David knew who to kill, knew where the fellow lived, some hotel. Once he did this deed he would leave the territory, put it well behind him.

He did not abide Kansas nor Kansans. Lawrence was invented by weird strangers from back East. These loud folk arrived with high-minded ideas and Yankee money, instructing Missourians like children. While he did not truck with irregulars who burn folks out in the night, by no means did he truck with busybodies.

Sun was soothing. He lay down on the matted grass and gazed at clouds. Looked peaceful, the sky, it was a fine day. He took in a deep breath of sweet-smelling air, nice and easy.

*   *   *

Fell into sleep, dreamed about Chickamauga, a squirrelly creek in North Georgia. He and his Tennessee Volunteers fought there a year after Shiloh. They had a good General then, Braxton Bragg, who David saw pass and who looked like a leader of men, a real soldier. Before the fight, the boys at camp were saying the union General was a dandy named Rosecrans, who truly did not know his hindquarters from a spit bucket. Sure enough, the next day, space opened up in the blue line because of poor deployment. The break was enough to charge a regiment through, and that's what the blond and his fellows did. Killed a lot of Ohioans that day, their blue blood ran red. Would have killed more, but union artillery got dragged into position on the high ground and let fly all sorts of hell, turning the tide of battle.

In the dream the Gray coats were attacking the blues' splintering lines, some union boys had already run like plain cowards. All of a sudden and most unexpectedly, Federal artillery commenced firing. Tremendous booming sounds, earth shaking, boy name of Todd nearby got hit with a solid cast iron shot. Damnedest thing: hit him square and ripped him into pieces didn't look human. The ball kept rolling, took a foot off a fellow, then killed a horse fixed to a buckboard. The artillery was also flinging canister and grape shot. It was raining iron plugs and lead, David passed a Missoura farmer named Cecil stretched on the ground like a scarecrow full of bloody shot.

That day at Chickamauga, the Grays would have chased the Yankees right out of Georgia except for that artillery. Later in camp the blond heard it was Germans from Ohio firing the field pieces. They were soldiers who didn't even speak English. He did not like Ohio or its people after that.

David woke up to the sound of Boy making a pleading noise that told him the horse was thirsty. He got up and led the animal away from the trees to the edge of the stream. Both horse and man bent down into the water for a drink. It was good, helpful, McClure's head was clearing. He got the notion that Boy understood he was having a bad dream, that dark memories were doing him no good. The horse started snorting just to wake him up. Another reason to admire that animal.

After the dreamy dullness cleared, David decided: he'd backtrack into town, do the one last deed, after all, he'd given his word. For safekeeping, he hid his greenbacks in a crevice covered with sprawling ivy.

*   *   *

Day later the blond stood on Main. He looked at the painted-green building across the street. Minerva Hotel, it said on a fancy sign. Unusual moniker, wonder what it meant? Knowing Kansans, didn't mean anything.

Did not feel good being in this town, the most Yankee town in the entire west. It was named after A.C. Lawrence, egghead do-gooder who founded the New England Emigrant Aid Company. Place was nothing when McClure he was a boy, they called the street main because it was the only street. 'Round then abolitionists arrived, declaring to folk that the land was a holy place. Pro-slavery, abolitionists, David did not rightly know what that talk meant. He hated the union, but not because of black folk. Back in the Pony Express, he knew a rider, Charley Bender, black as night. He was a bowlegged rider, a good one, a nice kid who was always smiling. When David started out in the war with the Missouri volunteers, there was a Negro cook who tagged along, name of Curly. A freedman, he always had beans and coffee ready in the evening. He was originally from Troy and he was a defender of his homeland.

Common opinion was that black men were stupid. In David's experience, he'd met whites more stupid than coloreds, though honestly Curly and Charley were both slow witted. The blond could despise men, but not on account of skin, had to be a real reason.

Abolitionists told other folk how to live, that was a reason. So when he heard the man to be kilt was an eastern professor, an abolitionist and a dastardly fellow to boot, he told himself it was okay.

He crossed the dusty street to the front of the hotel. Quiet enough. Folks were out and about, ladies with their parasols, buckboard rolled by, gents walking and talking. Nobody paying attention to a cowboy in *chaparajos*. He entered the Minerva. Little man behind the front desk was reading a newspaper real serious, pointing with a finger at the print. There was an old man sitting on the lobby's divan. He was smoking a pipe and mumbling to himself.

David knew to head up the staircase and he took it to the second floor. He eased down a carpeted hallway, past a couple rooms, keeping his Colt holstered. At the end of the hall, he reached a door ajar. He gave the portal a push and stepped inside. A man was sitting in a chair, reading a book. He looked up at David. The blond sniffed and stared him down.

"You Hedley?" he asked.

"And who are you?"

"A man with a gun." David had the drop on him, they considered each other. Blond had a thought cross his mind that this bookish fellow seemed young and steely-eyed for a professor. Then the man in the chair lifted his book and showed he was holding a black pistol, a Spiller & Burr, and the blond was thinking damn, that's a fine gun. At the same time, on his right, another man stepped from the other room. He was a squat fellow with a badge and an imposing Sharps.

McClure did not dare make a move. "You ain't Hedley," he said. The man got up, gun barrel leveled. Reaching with his other hand, he picked up a badge from the bookstand, pinned it to his vest.

"I am the Sheriff of Lawrence," he said.

The blond quick-put his right hand on the butt of his pistol, an instinct. At the same time, Slim jumped at him and swung a goodly leather cudgel, struck David square on the head, knocking him right out.

V

Connor Quinn was invariably larger than any acquaintance or stranger. So it came as a surprise when he visited a preacher as tall and several pounds fuller than he. The man was bald-pated, with a curled up moustache made him look like either a circus strongman or a dandy. The marshal had the urge to laugh at the sight, though he couldn't well snicker at a bible-toter. He shook the man's hand, gave him his best Irish smile: "Connor Quinn," was all he said.

Preacher held the hand in his meat hook. Not a smiler, he gave a grave nod. "Pleasure, name is Marion Harker, what can I do for you?"

Those were all the preliminaries these two would need. Pastor motioned to a chair and the lawman sat, tucking his riding coat behind a gold-plated Colt Walker. He took out a pouch from his coat and rolled a smoke as he parleyed.

"Reverend, I'm here to inquire about one of your sheep."

"Sheep."

"Man name of Chester Whitbread."

Harker took a long breath. "Yes," he said.

"You do know him?"

"I do."

"He's a rancher of means, business man, perhaps a personal friend of yours."

"Every man and woman in St. Joseph is my friend."

"That is a Christian attitude." Quinn looked around the room for no good reason, then continued: "About this Whitbread fellow. . ."

"Marshal, I regret to inform you that he is deccased."

The lawman could roll a smoke fast as you please. He was finished, had the thing in his mouth and now took it out. "My goodness, that a fact?" He acted taken aback.

"Passed away three days ago, we interred him yesterday over in Oakridge."

"I'm sorry to hear that news, the man is gone. What killed him may I ask?"

"He got sick, had a cancer, it was sudden, virulent, terrible shock to his family who are good people."

While listening, Quinn seemed sympathetic, though he wasn't one to carry off the performance. Then he threw a hand into the air, as if plain exasperated. There was a twinkle in his eye. "Have I ridden all the way from Kansas for naught?"

Harker was curt. "That is a long ride but perhaps you have."

"Really did want to talk to Boss, that's what they called him I understand."

"He was Boss, it was a term of endearment. His father before him was a true pioneer in these parts, and Chester cut a wide swath, family man and pillar of the community."

The marshal let a moment pass. "Reverend, may I light up?"

"Sir, be my guest. Would you prefer a cigar?"

"I would not, thanks." The lawman had a match out and struck against a nearby doorframe, though it was considered impolite to do such a thing in a stranger's home. The preacher was gracious and did not comment on the transgression.

"Mr. Quinn, do you often come to St. Joe?"

"I make it a habit not to, I was born and raised in great Kansas, do not frequent secession locales."

"Missouri was not a member of the confederacy."

"True, much politicking involved there. Were you in the border war?"

The pastor made a face at the choice of words. "Border war is a phrase concocted by ignorant farmers."

"Sorry, no disrespect meant."

"I fought in the war between the States."

"I hope you fought on the winning side."

"I did not."

"Nary a care, we're all Americans now."

"How about you, Marshal? Where did you serve?"

"I was a special case," he offered, took a drag, blew smoke, and said nothing more. Harker did not know what Quinn meant nor did he care. Any special case bought an unfortunate to serve in his place. The act was ungodly. Strange, this Kansas lawman seemed proud enough.

The reverend was direct. "Mr. Quinn, I assumed you knew of the passing of Whitbread. Our Sheriff Bailey wired Topeka concerning the diseased."

"Ah, your sheriff, a fine man though I have never had the pleasure of his acquaintance."

"Served the Union, excelled in the campaign against Mobile. Did you receive his telegram?"

"Well that's the thing, damn if my deputy didn't lose that. Chewed him out, don't you fret."

"We gave the name McClure as the criminal to be on the look-out for."

"Reverend, that outlaw is caught."

"Praise God."

"Two days ago in Lawrence. He is as good as hanged. Now, if I may come to the point of my visit after such a long ride: It is my understanding the dying man confessed to you."

"He spoke to me, we spoke of things."

"Confessed, spoke. I'm wondering what he might have said."

"I'm not sure what it is you mean."

"Well, for instance, regarding this outlaw and the dastardly plans."

"He unburdened his conscience, said he hired the cowboy."

"The cowboy, like I said, good as hung." Quinn put a hand to his throat, gave a rub, as if his words weren't clear enough. Then he got close to the Reverend and spoke confidential-like. "Am to understand that the boss was a sinner who unburdened his conscience, every sorry, criminal deed?"

Harker did not care for the way this man phrased his words. Still, he was a guest and thus entitled to patience. "He was a good man who made a terrible, misguided mistake," the host explained.

"Reverend, what I would like you to do, what I came this long way for, is for you to tell me if Whitbread mentioned others involved in the scheming." There was something about the insistent lawman, sitting with one leg crossed over the other and blowing smoke into the air. It was like he knew the answers but inquired nonetheless, like it was all a child's game.

Preacher did not appreciate the style. "I informed Sheriff Bailey of what Whitbread told me about McClure. The Boss was dying and rightly wanted to clear his conscience before heaven's glory. His exact words I cannot say to you."

"Why is it you cannot say?"

"He confessed to me as a man of the Lord."

"Alright, did not know it worked like that."

"Are you a churchgoer, Marshal?"

"Sadly no, occupied serving the people of Kansas."

Harker could only nod. "In regards to what you came for, I would direct your further concerns to the law here in St. Joe. And now, if you will excuse me, I have a sermon to prepare and other business." Pastor also had a way about him. He stood over the Kansan and looked down in a manner frankly frightening. Quinn was thinking that if Harker was not a preacher, he'd have made a fine gun. "What's the sermon on?" the marshal inquired as he got up from his seat.

"Greed, Road to Hell."

"Sounds inspirational and depressing," the marshal offered. Preacher walked to the door of the room, opened it, and stood there. Quinn laughed for no reason. He might have made more of the situation but the hulking man in front of him seemed the size of a locomotive and just as revved. So the marshal picked up his hat, placed it on his head, and departed.

He trudged down creaking stairs, out the front door of the cottage, and walked through the yard to Peach Tree Lane. There, three of his deputies were waiting with horses near some poplars. The men were a sight with their riding coats flapping in the wind, badges and gun butts shining in the sun's glare. The Marshal motioned to one of them, dark fellow with a moustache name of Jackson, who wore handguns holstered on either side. Quinn waved a come hither. Jackson strode to him.

"Nice town, St. Joseph," Quinn opined insincerely.

The man was the silent sort, barely moved a muscle in his face when he spoke. "Tain't bad," he uttered.

"Why don't you stay a spell, lay low, ears open."

"Yes sir," Jackson replied.

"Best you take off that coat and badge."

Quinn walked away, mounted his palomino, and rode down the lane with the other deputies. They reached Main. Townsfolk couldn't help but notice the Kansans; everybody knew who they were. The marshal reared his mount up upon its hind legs for effect, the animal neighed and the rider gave it a slap to steady it.

Quinn then gazed up at a window in a building that housed the Firebird saloon. There was a redheaded gal, likely a whore, watching, her arms folded across her waist. What in tarnation was she looking at?

*   *   *

Smith was well acquainted with duty. His life was informed by strict principles and the clear understanding of his obligations, whether they were to his family, friends, country, or to his God. He was single minded when it came to that. One to allow his actions to speak louder than mere words, now was the test of those life-long convictions.

He was at a rough-hewed cedar table, attired in a newly pressed suit. The sun through the window cast a shadow that divided the tabletop. In sunshine laid a shotgun of double barrel. It was a Winchester, from a company of that name back east in New Haven, Connecticut.

Smith had taken the weapon apart and was now cleaning with a rag dampened with light lamp oil. Barrels, stock, cocking slide, extractor, firing pin, he took his meticulous time. Long, bony but strong fingers held each piece in the light; he rubbed the rag, working surfaces, he blew at dust. Finished, he reassembled Mainspring, hammer spring, latch spring, he knew guns like bookish men know letters. Just as the Winchester was reassembled, his wife entered the room. Her name was Becca, she was a slim woman of sharp features and kind eyes. Now her countenance portrayed concern. Leaning against the doorway's frame, she seemed real serious.

"Jacob," was what she said. In response, he did not look up but wore a rueful smile. She rubbed her own arms as she held them at her waist. "Never too many guns," she stated to suggest joking. He neither laughed nor smiled.

"Becca, the task is at hand, this weapon is for that purpose."

"When you say at hand, you mean the goings on with the Boss."

He was surprised by her words, seemed she knew more than he had told her. He nodded yes. He set the Winchester down and stood with her. What a fine woman. God fearing, supportive, with a lovely smile. How blessed he was.

Jacob Smith was a man unlike others. He did not approve of the Boss's course of action, but that did not change what was owed. He promised Chester Whitbread he would do a thing, a last job, and it would be difficult and dangerous. Boss had aided his family during the war, when the Whitbread clan was spared over-much hardship and the Smiths were not, got him up and on his feet after the damnable war. Now payback was nigh, simple as that.

Seeking to reassure to wife, he embraced her. "Dear, you are of delicate constitution, you mustn't fret or it will do you ill."

Wife, a smart woman, listened quietly, and she knew he loved her. She wanted to say so many things to her husband, finally she spoke. "It's a long way to Kansas. Be especially careful."

He was taken aback, how did she know where he was going? Jacob turned away from his beloved. She left the room with tears welling, went to their bed. He felt poorly hearing his wife's sobs. Still tears could not deter him.

He had the cleaned-and-ready shotgun on the table. Also there was a long white cardboard box. He set it next to the gun. Then he took something out of his coat pocket. It was a shiny green ribbon and bow. He placed the shotgun in the box and wrapped it up with the ribbon. Looked real nice.

*   *   *

The man at the telegraph office, name of Thistle, made a face and read the page again. He wasn't the best reader in the county. He checked the dots and dashes from his teleprinter to be certain he'd transcribed the impulses correctly. Satisfied, he left the office on Maple Street in St. Joseph, hurried around the corner to the town's newspaper, The Missouri Star. Thistle held the telegram folded at his side so as not to attract attention. After all, he had to go past the paper's publisher whose office was at the front of the first floor, past the editor who had an office in the back, then up a flight of stairs to the second floor. There he found a reporter named Ben DeCamp, who had started working at the paper not so long ago.

What would *he* be doing getting a confidential message from Thomas Powell, Sheriff of Lawrence? Didn't make sense, didn't have to. Thistle did what telegraph office employees do.

"Howdy, Ben," he announced as he arrived at a room with an oval window facing the street.

"Thistle," came a smiling reply. The reporter was a small-framed man, but fit and strong. He had a full head of wavy brown hair and wore wire-framed spectacles. He took them off now and faced the visitor. "What have you got there?" he inquired.

"Telegram from Lawrence Kansas."

"Sure it's for me?"

65

"Sure as shootin', your name is right here, first thing." He handed over the paper. The reporter put his specs back on and read the telegram. He looked up at the messenger, then read the telegram again. "I'd like to send a reply," he said.

Thistle was nothing if not prepared. Lickety-split he had writing paper and the stub of a pencil. He brought the pencil to his mouth to wet the tip.

"Ready and able," he said.

"Captain, received your message, will do, DeCamp," he dictated as Thistle jotted.

"*Captain*, what's that all about?"

"My friend, it's about you writing that down and sending it."

"Fine and dandy," Thistle stated, taking not the least offense. He tucked the message into a pocket and marched out the way he came.

VI

Jail in Lawrence was a harsh place. In a part of town that was burned by Quantrill, it had been rebuilt quickly with nary a care for beauty nor comfort. The walls were logs laid atop another, chips and moss filling gaps. There was a sizable oak table in a corner, rack of rifles hung next to it. A board of men-wanted posters adorned the other wall. Besides that, a potbelly stove, two bare, wooden chairs, a smaller table, and a spittoon were all there was up front.

Halfway across began the bars of the cells, three cells in all. The back wall was stone, assuring that accommodations were damp and drafty. This was fine with Powell. The drunks, gamblers and troublemakers who merited a night in jail deserved no better. All this is to say it was most certainly a proper place for a killer of men.

David woke, flat on his back. Initial thoughts were that getting caught in that professor's hotel room was a weird dream. He stared at the ceiling, where drops of condensation gathered. One fell and hit his chest, that's when full awareness dawned. He'd been caught. He had a pounding headache from the cudgel's blow, now he felt the lump atop his head, there was some dried blood.

He thought about his horse, Boy. What happened to the animal, tethered as it was outside that hotel? It wouldn't still be there; lawmen were good about that, wouldn't lose a man's horse, even when they'd hang the rider.

He sat up in the bunk, shook his head clear. Spotted a lean, dark haired man at the desk, writing with a pencil. Man wore a badge; it was the sheriff, the one who said he was the bookish Hedley. McClure got up and came to the front of his cell. The sheriff considered him, neither said a word. The prisoner had both his hands on iron bars.

"You look passing familiar," the blond finally stated.

"You too," Thomas answered.

67

"Why's that?"

"We both were riders for the Pony Express."

David got a look like fog lifted. "My station was St. Joe," he said.

"Mine Sacramento," came the answer that explained why the two had never properly met, they rode in opposite directions, home bases being fifteen hundred miles apart. There were eighty riders in the express, one hundred stations and five hundred horses. Likely as not, the two knew men who knew each other, maybe they even passed in western Kansas or northern Colorado and gave a wave.

Powell got up from his desk and approached the prisoner.

"They called you Davey."

"Name is David, like in the Bible."

"Other riders called you Davey. I knew Calvin Beauchamp, he knew you."

"Beauchamp, maybe, don't recall. What did they call you?"

The sheriff looked down, got embarrassed. "Silly name, dispatcher gave me."

"Which dispatcher?"

"Fellow named Simon Shanks."

"Man with a great long beard."

"Him."

"What did he call you?"

"Hard Ride."

The blond let out a sound, almost a laugh. "Hard Ride, skinny kid who jumped off his mount fancy. You got taller, put on some weight. You got a real name?"

"Thomas Powell." The blond said nothing. The sheriff moved to the potbelly stove and fetched a cup of coffee. He offered it and it was accepted.

The prisoner had a sip. It was lousy, fitting the entire situation. He looked at the sheriff hard. "How did you catch me?" he asked. The lawman was not one to gab with a wanted man. But this was different.

68

"You were betrayed," the lawman began, "It was found out you would be in Lawrence and who you were to harm." The blond had heard "betrayed." He was pretty sure he knew what that word meant.

"Be-trayed," he said as if it was two words. "Who did it?"

"The man who hired you."

David was incredulous. "No way, not that fat man. He had big plans."

"Strange I know, but he was dying and wanted to fess up."

"Boss is dead."

"As can be, cancer killed him."

The blond looked down at the dirty floor of the cell. "That is the chance you take believing what folks tell you," he stated like it was all expected and all bad. He thought about his horse. "Where's my mount?" he asked.

"At the corral," the sheriff answered.

"They know what they're doing down there, taking care of animals?"

"They do."

"The horse likes a good rubdown."

"Ned Tyrel will attend to it."

"And he don't cotton to a cramped berth, needs stomping room."

"Ned has boys walk the horses."

"What happens to it after I hang?"

"Gets sold I suppose."

McClure grabbed the bars of the cell door firmly. "Can't have that, horse won't let anyone else ride it." After the outburst, he pushed away, sat back down on his bunk.

Sheriff judged the prisoner awfully worked up over an animal. "I wouldn't fret, he's freer than you," he confirmed.

*   *   *

The blond considered his situation. Hanging was a certainty, Kansas or Missoura, wherever the law decided. He never imagined hanging would be his end. If the fall from the gallows didn't snap a neck, the tightening rope chokes off breath. If he had his druthers, the end would come as a frail old man, white haired and toothless, in bed with a buxom gal. Fact was the path he trod likely led to a harsh destiny. Shootout, guns ablaze, hope to die quick in that case. Swinging at the end of a rope, on the other hand, was shameful, suited for cowards.

He wondered what this lawman knew, the pony rider who caught him. He watched as Thomas took down a wanted poster and put up another one. Something about him, a look told you he was capable, there was no mistaking a leader of men.

"I figure you were a Yankee," the prisoner called out.

The sheriff turned and held his hand up, like he wanted something clear.

"Don't call me Yankee. There were unionists and Rebels. I wore blue."

"I wore gray."

"I know you did."

"You have a rank?"

"Captain, by the end."

"An officer, I would've guessed. Missoura Volunteers went by two ranks, dead and alive."

"You were at Shiloh?"

"Yep, you?"

"Yep."

"Don't believe I saw you out there, but you must have been a real soldier to survive that fight."

"Weren't many of us at the end, we backed off when we were told to."

"Good thing for you, Hard Ride, was easy to die that day." He offered a toast of his coffee: "We both outlived a war." Powell did not return the sentiment. David was a canny one, even as he was sincere in wishing his jailer well, he eyed the gun rack hung on the wall. That was a fine Wesson on the top rung.

He spoke up. "You and me are alike, Sheriff, both pony-ridin' fighters."

Thom put his cup down hard. "We are not alike, McClure. I wear a badge; you kill folks."

"You kill alright." Powell did not rightly know what his prisoner meant by those words, he would not answer them. The man behind the bars continued, "A while back I heard barroom chatter about the Sheriff of Lawrence killing bank robbers, Hell, I heard you kilt William Quantrill."

Thomas said nothing until he stated "I engage in gunfire when duty requires. Far as Quantrill, it's true I fought in his last fight."

"Met his end not far from here, I do believe."

"He did. You ride with him?"

"Quantrill?"

"That's what I'm asking." The prisoner got red in the face; Powell knew McClure was insulted, which was the intention.

"I was a regular soldier like my fellows. Didn't ride at midnight with a torch," David said. He was shaking the bars of his cell, like that could do some good. Sheriff came over to his prisoner, eye to eye.

"You take offense at my words? I take offense you come to my town intending harm to a good man, for no good reason far as I can see."

"That fellow deserved it," is what David said. Then his face changed, like he knew those words bore no weight. Came into his mind to lie, and though the blond was not by nature a teller-of-tales, he gave it a try.

"I owed money from a game of poker, that's why I agreed to do the deed. Ain't proud of it."

Thomas could tell the lie, though the blond was cool. It was perplexing and passing strange, McClure was a man who could kill, but not lie well. So Thom kept at it: "After the war you should've been making a new life, with a gal."

David gave a look. "Mister, where did you end up at war's end? Where I was there were dead-end folks, meal a day for the fortunate. Far as a gal goes, I have one, redhead in St. Joe, thinks the world of me."

The blond got a far-away look, knowing the talk was empty. He waved his hand in the air for no plain reason. But David wasn't finished talking. "You been making a new life, Powell? You got a girl?"

Thom left his prisoner to awful coffee and he sat back at his desk. He would not speak of Baili in the presence of a killer of men.

*　　　*　　　*

A matron, Dorothy Lysander, sat at the organ playing "All My Strength Lord Comes from Thee." Least that's what the congregation fancied the song was, as Dorothy, though sweet, was not much of a player and the hymn's notes wandered some. Thomas had strolled into Sunday service with Baili, made a point of walking up the center aisle to the first row of seats. All the churchgoers saw, every last Christian, each free to draw their conclusions. Thomas and Baili greeted the preacher, man name of Buttle, who smiled and gave a welcoming bow. Pastor Buttle was one of the founders of the town; an old-time abolitionist who was acquaintance of John Brown himself. Preacher had seen his place of worship burned five years back by the Rebel non-believers. He was a straight talking, high-minded gent. Wouldn't object in the least to a Chinese woman's arm slipped under a white man's, especially this man.

The congregation sang, "Meet me in Heaven." Baili held the song-card in front of her, reading words, seemed she knew the tune. She sang in a soft voice, barely audible. Then she intoned a verse in a strange language Thom figured was Chinese, which he had never heard spoke. Then at the chorus, she sang in English with the others that we will all meet in heaven. He looked sideways at her, baffled and intrigued.

After the service, the two left last. They were content sitting in the pew until Pastor Buttle escorted them outside where the flock was gathered on Oak Street. Baili was a picture of quiet dignity. Her arm gently on his, head held high, though not so much as to suggest pride.

Thomas was thinking it was a fine Sunday.

*   *   *

Around that time, with gray clouds filling the wide sky, Jacob Smith rode into Lawrence on a Paint. Dressed in a black suit and overcoat, he held across his saddle a long box with a green ribbon. He came in from the east, into Vermont and then Main. Past the green grocer's, the general store and apothecary, past a rundown saloon with a strange name, "Belongs to Me." Mount ambled in a wavering gait, like the rider wasn't eager to reach any destination.

Soon enough, there was the sheriff's office. Smith eased up, dismounted, and tethered at the rail. He walked up the steps, the box held under one arm. He stopped at the doorframe and looked up and down the quiet-enough street. No reason to wait a moment longer. His hat was pulled low and his collar was turned up around his face, rendering his visage nigh unrecognizable.

Jacob was feeling peculiar. It was like his sum past had arrived at that doorframe, like the moments tethering his Paint just now were the most important of his life. What a puzzling notion. He fought his own mind not to make much of it. He thought of Becca and that settled him.

Smith turned the knob and stepped in. Saw two deputies in front. In the back there was a prisoner in a cell. Slim was sitting at the desk, had his feet up. Red was standing next to the row of cells, having a smoke. The visitor took a look at the two, nodded, and cast a glance to the man in the first cell, who was pressed against the stone wall. David leaned forward, recognizing the Boss's gun straight away, turned-up collar notwithstanding.

Slim got off his chair. "Good day, stranger, you're all bundled up I see," he offered. Smith closed the door behind him and stood holding the box. Red looked him up and down, took the smoke out of his mouth.

"Undertaker's around the corner, third building in," he giggled. Slim guffawed, then waved Red away.

73

"Don't mind him, mister."

"I don't mind him." the stranger said.

"What can we do for you?"

Smith, never a man of words, saw no reason for them now. He took the box he was holding and laid it on the desk in front of Slim.

"Nice ribbon, what is it?" the deputy asked innocently.

With that, Smith reached out and flicked at the ribbon, loosening it. He flipped open the lid of the box. There was the Winchester, ready to go. He took it and aimed at the men.

"Make nary a move, gents," the gunman began, "No need for any man to get himself buck shot today," Smith had the lawmen dead to rights. It should have been easy at that point. He would spring McClure, lock the hapless deputies in a cell, and be off. Smith had promised the Boss to do that, give the cowboy one chance to run for it, seeing as the blond had been betrayed.

Soundest plans can unfold badly and this one did. With the black barrel of the shotgun between the deputies, Slim did something ill-advised. Aspiring to out-quick the stranger, he backhanded the long gun up toward the ceiling. Problem was Slim was jumpy and unable to grab a hold.

Shotgun jerked. One barrel discharged with a roaring, resounding boom. Slim did not get hit head-on, that would have killed him sure. Instead, a line of pellets raked him waist to shoulder. Off his feet he flew into the wall, against the gun rack which fell on top of him. Roar echoed greatly and filled the room's air with pungent smoke. Slim attempted to squeeze off a pistol shot, though he was mightily unbalanced. The gun made a sharp pop sound. However, all he did was blow off the tip of his own boot. Acquiescing to his dire condition, he dropped the gun in pain and blood.

Smith wheeled the Winchester at Red, who was pronouncing "damn" over and again. McClure was at the door of the cell, shaking the bars to beat the band. Red fumbled at his Colt Walker, by then the shotgun was pointed right at 'im.

Smith's look was grim, confessing that events were out of control. He was going to have to kill or be killed if he was to finish what he started. Yet he was a God fearing man, not a natural killer. His plan was to shoot the legs out from under the man going for his Walker.

Smith had the plan but Red had the purest luck, and luck trumped. The trigger of the shotgun was squeezed, click. Nothing, the damn gun misfired. In a moment Smith dropped it on the desk where it landed with a thud. He reached across his body for the pistol in his waistband. By this time Red had steadied his gun. The two fired blam blam. More roaring smoke filled the room. Red got hit in the gut. He let out a grunt, grabbed the hole in his stomach with a fist, and fell back against the iron bars of the cell.

Still Red was awfully lucky because his own gunshot was wild high. The lead struck the brass lampshade affixed to the ceiling. Shot of lamentable destiny: the ricochet hit clean into Jacob Smith's chest and heart. The surprised gunman let out a sound, like the air in his lungs got sucked. Looking down at the smoking hole in his suit, he ripped at his shirt. Thoroughly forlorn, he spun as he stood, falling over, hitting the wooden, well-trod floor, face first.

David knew what to do. He grabbed the gut-shot deputy through the bars of his cell and he took the jailer's keys. Across the room, Slim was making low noises, half his body stained with slow-flowing blood. Also bleeding dark red was his foot. The errant shot had not only ruined his boot, but taken a toe or two. The blond unlocked the cell, the opening door pushing Red, moaning and belly bleeding, aside. David stood amidst the wounded, sizing up their situation. "You'll both live," he announced, having previously seen enough shot men to make the call.

Meantime Smith was real dead. He was stretched out on the jailhouse floor, a bullet hole clean through his outer coat and pressed jacket.

David bent over the man who sprung him. Damnedest thing, the blond couldn't even inquire why he did what he did. No time to contemplate, first thing he fetched was his knives, he'd seen his jailers place them in the desk drawer. Then he picked up Red's Walker, recognizing a fine weapon. Clumsy lawman didn't deserve it. He could have taken Smith's mint-condition Winchester but he witnessed the misfire, the weapon couldn't be trusted. Instead, he grabbed a Springfield repeater rifle from the shattered rack, plus four boxes of shells, two for each gun.

McClure stood in the middle of the blood and death and stinking vapors and listened: commotion outside; dogs barking, he knew it wouldn't be long before men with guns came running to see who was shooting up the sheriff's office. At the front door, he looked out and saw two citizens in the street pointing at him through the window. He ran to the back and out the alley.

*   *   *

Still outside the church on Oak, Thom found himself reluctantly conversing on the coming planting season. He and Baili had been buttoned-holed by a farmer who was either passionate about crops or wanted a closer look at the Chinese girl.

That was when the distant discharge of a booming gun shattered Sunday's calm. There followed pistol shots, pop, pop. That was enough. Thomas nodded "Reverend," to the preacher, turned to Baili. He touched the tip of his hat, gave her the lightest kiss to her cheek. Then he ran full bore to the sound of guns, her eyes followed his flight.

*   *   *

David was moving too, down the alley to Fork Street, running parallel to Main. He was heading for the corral. As it was the Lord's Day, it was quiet about. He scurried past one house. There a citizen, lifting a window's curtain, spotted him. Then the curtain dropped at the sight of a fierce man carrying weapons in each hand.

Escapee reached the corral on the run. There was the gent the sheriff called Ned standing in front. He reached for his pistol,

76

but stopped when the blond had his gun directed at him before he could take another breath.

"Live or die, up to you," David called out and Ned knew he meant it, hands went up over his head after he dropped his weapon into the dust.

"Where's Boy?"

"Boy?"

"The animal."

"Animal?"

"My damn horse." Ned made a nervous motion with his arm. David looked to the stalls and saw his mount. Just like that he flipped his revolver and holstered it, then took the rifle, turned it stock up, and smacked Ned on the side of the head real hard, knocked him down and out. Blond could hear voices, yelling, dogs barking, and he knew the capable sheriff would be arriving.

David figured right then that time had run out for both him and his horse. He approached Boy, who was snorting and jumping against the stall in recognition of its master, then steadied itself. David held the horse's head and patted. He heard more yelling from outside.

"Sorry Boy," he said in a cold voice, "can't go with me this last hard ride." With that he took out his revolver, cocked it.

*   *   *

There was a fellow in town, Nathan Farnsworth. Had been a deputy for Sheriff Powell. He got married months back and decided he'd rather care for his woman, raise children, tend farm, than be deputy, understandable. Now he stood with Thomas on the platform at the train depot just as the *780* came shushin' and hissin' into the station. This was first thing Monday. Thom turned to Nathan. "I want to thank you for your service," he said as the two shook hands.

Farnsworth was of average height, a broad-shouldered, muscular man. Not a fellow to ever wear a hat, he had long, brown hair down to his shoulders, a weather-beaten face. Held a right hand on the butt of his pistol, and waved at the train's engineer as the iron horse pulled in. Nathan wore a badge. "Glad to help, Captain," he said, "Terrible day in Lawrence yesterday."

It had been: two deputies shot, their lives balancing between the skill of a doctor and the will of the Lord. Yesterday had seen a stranger killed dead helping a prisoner escape; one corral owner with a busted head, a dead horse. Baffling events that compelled Thomas into action. Now he bid adieu at the platform, boarded the train, and settled into his seat in the last car.

He pondered the previous day's events. When he entered his office on the run, gun drawn, he was greeted by carnage. Slim had been struck by shotgun discharge and was unconscious. The left side of his body full of pellets, bleeding a good bit, clothes all tore up. Odd thing, there was a fancy green ribbon across his chest. Far as Red, he was shot but conscious, holding his belly real tight though that did not stanch the flow. McClure's cell was empty.

"I think I winged 'im," Red grunted and pointed. Across the room a man seemed to be kissing the floor. His spreading blood told the story.

"You winged him alright," Powell answered. The corpse owned a Winchester and a Le Mat revolver. Seemed that here was a gunman who got the drop on deputies and sprung a prisoner. Got himself kilt in the deal.

*   *   *

Alone in a back car on the 8 wheeler *780*, Thomas took stock of the situation. McClure had shot his own horse. Why would he do that, shoot an animal that he had shown particular concern for? Made some sense if the prisoner planned a real hard ride figuring it would kill the creature. Riding a horse to death is a terrible end for the animal, so the outlaw did it quick. It was sixty miles Lawrence to St. Joseph. If McClure rode one mount hard that distance, he would kill it for sure. It would be the hefty price paid for a man's will to survive. McClure had a will honed in war, a driven gift. Anyway you reckoned, it was more than passing strange.

While a posse of capable men was already after the outlaw, Thom had a hunch that he would follow on his own. Sheriff judged his fellow pony rider single-minded. McClure had mentioned a gal he fancied, a redhead in St. Joe. That's where Tom would go. Come what may, the lawman was prepared for any tussle. He was carrying his trusted Spiller & Burr, but also his five shot Paterson, seeing as it brought him luck that day at the Federal Bank. Into his boot he'd slid a silver-handled throwing knife, just in case. In the pockets of his jacket he had boxes of shells for both guns, and to top it off a trusted Colt carbine lie in the seat next to him. If there was a fight, he was ready.

*   *   *

With the train out of Lawrence picking up speed, on a flat stretch of Kansas east of town, Thom leaned back and lowered the brim of his hat down over his eyes. The rails made a clank-clanking sound. The monotony of it was soothing. He must have been weary because he dozed.

In a dream he found himself at the Sunken Road. The trees were thick, there were tough cedars where Corporal Powell and his unit were set. Across from them was a wide, flat field and a peach orchard.

It was early in the morn, Rebs were coming, at first barely discernible. There they were, grey ghosts emerging from morning mist. The corporal could see puffs of smoke, shots from the Tennessee boys, a half-dozen at a time, going off in a group with a pop pop; then came the crashing of Minie balls into the cedars of the tree line, a God awful sound. Pieces of wood commenced flying wild from wounded trees. A ball hit an officer two men away from him, a gut wound. The man was down and bellowing, though he couldn't be heard over the bustle of battle. Thom judged his fellows panicky, firing back too soon, wasting precious breath cursing the enemy. Let 'em come, let 'em get close enough to shoot at proper.

His weapon was an army-issue Colt rifle, good enough. Now the Grays were closing in, Rebel yelling like they do. Thom turned to men with him, calling out "hold boys, hold steady." He had brought his rifle up from where he knelt into a natural notch in a tree trunk. He held his breath then squeezed. Hit a Reb solid, the man grabbed his thigh, crashed to the ground onto bramble. Thom readied his breech loader, aimed and fired. Another Gray-coat was struck, both the man's arm and his weapon were shattered.

That's when the sheriff woke with a start. He couldn't have been asleep for more than a minute. It was longer: the *780* was steaming into St. Joe station.

VII

David stood in the hallway. He knocked on the door, giving the wood two quick raps. She opened the portal and a blank look turned into a sweet smile.

"I knew it was you," she said, though she couldn't have known. She pulled him into the room. He was a haggard sight, with dusty clothes and a wild tangle of hair. "You look like you been riding all night," she said.

He was silent though glad to see her. He crossed to the window, parted the curtain with care, and looked down at the street. It was quiet. He was limping, she noticed. "What's with your leg, darling?" she asked in a concerned voice.

It was just his horse collapsing and falling on him a mile or so out of town. The animal died right there, panting and dry heaving then silent. Horses make a screeching noise when deeply pained, damnedest sound. The rider felt pity for the creature but not over-much. He figured he was next and would suffer his own pain.

Now, dirty and tired, David grabbed her thin, cool arms. He pulled her close. "You mean the things you say to me?" he inquired. She got wide eyed like a child being asked "Are you a good girl?"

"Yes," she answered him. His eyes were fierce, like something inside wanted out. She didn't *get* this one. She relaxed in his arms, tossed her hair back.

"Why don't you ride me for a while?" she asked. She smelled like flowers. David wanted her but he knew time was short.

"Get dressed, there's a train leaving."

"Train, where we going?"

"Away."

"Honey, nothing would be better, but I have a job."

"You said you don't want to do this forever, how about you stop doing this now? I have money."

81

Neither said anything after that. She blinked at him with some uncertainty, finally she spoke in a soft voice: "You serious?"

David had not been sure of much in his young life: "You coming?" Her blushing face broke into a girlish laugh. "I am coming," she said, just as there was a knock on room's door.

"That must be Anna from downstairs, but don't you worry, I will explain that I am unavailable." The soon-to-be former whore opened the door some and peered, even as David took a step back. He had a feeling.

The blond saw the expression on her face, same time he saw the appearing barrel of a pistol raised in the door frame. The door opened wider. David reached to pull the girl away, there was no time. Gun went off with a sick boom that echoed in the room and seemed to shake the walls. The redhead got shot, went crashing back.

"I got one, I got one," shooter said in a voice betrayed by fear. David could see the gun barrel shaking, even as smoke curled from the tip. Meanwhile the girl whose name he never knew was flat on her back and dead as could be.

A second, stronger, voice came from the hallway. "You did not get one, you damn fool, you shot the whore." David understood the first voice was a deputy, the other the town's sheriff. The blond had his Colt drawn. Dark feelings rose quick from inside, an overwhelming force. He stepped forward with killing intent.

There was a whoosh sound and just like that the deputy, Clyde, got stuck clean through the throat with a thrown knife. The thick, bloody tip came out one side of his neck. He let out a sound, *gakk*. Dropped his pistol to the floor and clutched his throat. McClure squeezed the Colt's trigger, hit the gagging deputy. The foolish boy got sent backwards, leaking blood.

Sheriff Baily let out a yell, drew his gun, and pushed the dying man aside. The lawman was savvy, but no match for the fury he faced. The blond threw his second knife with his left hand, same time he fired remaining shots. Not only was the lawman hit with pieces of lead, he was stuck by the knife. All this before he could squeeze the trigger on his pistol but once, coming close to McClure but hitting wallboard.

Sheriff Bailey's hat fell, his arms went limp, and he dropped hard against the wall in the hallway. He tried to prop himself up to no avail, he slide down the wainscoting, expiring by the time he settled to the floor. He'd been a fine looking fellow in life, now his countenance was deathly calm.

Nobody left to kill, David took in a breath of air mixed with gunshot smoke. He walked back into the room and gazed at the dead girl. Still looked good, except for the right side of her face. He felt sadness and anger, the power of it tearing him up. He wished she was still alive and that the two of them were making their way to the train, were settled into their seats, and then were admiring the view of the prairie as the iron horse clanked along.

He removed two thrown knives from bodies, he'd need those blades. By now there was shouting and commotion from downstairs. Nothing else for McClure to do but head down the hallway to an open window, leaving behind the only person in his entire life to ever tell him he was good.

*   *   *

Outside the *bordello* at the Firebird, folks were reacting to the shots fired. Including Jackson the deputy. He was in a nearby eatery enjoying steak and eggs. He heard the commotion, stepped outside, and closed in on the Firebird. Most cautious, he stopped at a doorway, so he could get a look and still stay hid.

There was the blond across the alley, moving toward the street. The badge-less lawman could have done something at that point. He was not inexperienced, in fact he was a fast draw and strapped at his sides were pearl-handled six-shooters.

Jackson wanted to confront the crazy killer from Missoura to see what he was made of. But he had heard the gunfire; the sheriff, a capable man, was now full of holes. Who knew who else was kilt? Jackson would not test the firebrand. He skulked in shadows as the blond made his way.

*   *   *

It was ten in the morn and Thomas noted the tardiness. Suspicion arose and hung in the air as he waited in the office. He was told that the sheriff and his deputy would be back directly. Day before, Thom had sent a telegram. A wanted man, a killer, had escaped Lawrence's jail and run for St. Joe.

Now Powell paced the floor of creaky planks, certain that danger was nigh. He held in his hand a bullet, nothing special, he turned it over and again in his fingers, a nervous thing. Interminable moments passed, then a short and round man entered the office from the street, he was in a real rush. He had ruddy cheeks and was out of breath. He wore the pallor of the ill.

"Sheriff's shot," he panted, "Clyde is shot too."

That's how Thomas found out that two lawmen ran into outlaw David McClure. It got worse when Thomas learned who the dead sheriff was. None other than Charles T. Bailey, former Brigadier General in the union army and engineer by trade who had earned *Thanks of Congress* for his actions during the war. Thom did not know the man except by reputation, but it was painful to contemplate surviving a war and then dying in a bawdyhouse shootout.

He hated David McClure right then. When he learned a redheaded gal was shot along with the rest, he understood better. The outlaw had found himself in a situation, kill or be kilt. Damnable results.

After the tragic occurrences, there wasn't much for Thom to do in Missouri. McClure had left after the gunplay, ran down a side street and disappeared. He must have stolen a horse. In any case he'd leave a faint trail, here was a man used to running for his life.

*   *   *

Powell made his way down Maple Street to the Missouri Star, where he found Ben DeCamp in his office. There he was at his desk, old friend, bent over a piece of paper with a stub of a pencil. He idly hummed. The sight of him brought home right strong memories. Thom cleared his throat at the doorway, and the man looked up.

"Captain Powell," he said in joyful surprise. Thomas stepped into the room and the two shook hands, embraced, and backslapped.

"Haven't been called that in ages," Tom said with a laugh though it wasn't true. "It's good to see you."

"Likewise, terrible news in town today."

"Terrible, didn't know your sheriff was Charles Bailey."

"He was, a fair man, and a good fighter. Killer must have gotten the drop on him."

"Something went bad, that's certain."

"Sit if you please, take a load off." DeCamp poured his former commander a cup of coffee that tasted badly, just like during the war.

"So my friend, how have you been?" Thom inquired.

"Not a complaint, I am fit and have gainful employment. Funny a Kansas boy winding up in Missouri."

"It's a funny thing."

"Fish out of water as they say."

"The war was about freedom, they say that too."

DeCamp lit a thin cigar. "Will you be riding with the posse?"

"I will not. Truth is, I have my own ideas about McClure, which is the reason I sent you that telegram." Ben nodded affirmative and opened a drawer in his desk. From it he took a hand-written page.

"You are wondering about the men McClure kilt, I have some information." The reporter hesitated, as if waiting for an order to proceed. Old habits die hard. Thomas gave a wave.

"It was a month ago back in Seneca, first was Richard Stoddert, town elder. He was a railroad man who left the business, and he was active in local Indian charities. Man drowned in the Platte was one Henry Ambrose Hardee, former Vice President of the Hays Railroad Company. Henry opened and ran an orphanage through the graces of his church. Finally, fellow got shot on his buckboard outside of St. Joe here. Basil Early, owned a general store and a corral on Pine Street. He was said to be a charitable man, was with the Burlington Railroad before the war."

The sheriff wore a serious countenance. "Railroad men and do-gooders," he offered.

"What fight would McClure have with them?"

"McClure was a hired gun and we'll get 'im. Those who hire are killers sure as doers of deeds."

Ben puffed on the cigar, thinking, then he spoke. "Fact is railroads been giving land away, it's all the talk. Federals turned it over to them. Land means money thus harsh words and bad feelings. Around the border States men kill over such things."

It was a credible notion, made Powell believe this story was not simple. "Did any of these unfortunate men know each other?" he asked softly, like to himself. He cast a gaze down the long, dank hallway. He was not a gambling man, still he stated in sure tones, "I'll wager that they did."

*　　*　　*

Thomas found himself gladly back in Lawrence, at the Dwighton House for Ladies. He had come to visit Baili and he was uncertain as to how he might be received. He had been gone a week, seemed longer. Would she be glad to see him? He got his answer straight off, when she appeared at the top of the stairs, waved happily, and made her way down with an urgency that touched him.

She stood in his shadow, her eyes shown. "Hello Thomas."

He was soft-spoken. "Hello Baili, I am back." She nodded at his words. They had a sweet embrace. First thing she did was inquire as to his well-being with danger afoot. Even when he assured her, she looked him over to see for herself. She took his hand and turned him around, checked his clothes, even checked his boots. At that point he figured she was pulling his leg and they had a laugh.

*　　*　　*

They strolled Main to the edge of town. There was a garden there that marked a homestead burned by the irregulars in sixty-three. A cooling breeze lifted the smell of jasmine. Baili was inquisitive, so he told her about St. Joe, McClure, and the others. He shared enough to satisfy her curiosity but not more than she needed to know.

They stopped under the shade of poplars with a view of neat rows of lily blossoms and flowering bushes. He looked into her face, the visage was innocent and wise, impossible. He brushed hair away from her cheek. He could smell her skin. They kissed. Lips touched, barely, then pressed. It was wonderful. They separated, each a half-step back. He could tell she was pleased, and she must have known he was. He felt about as fine as he ever had. She slipped her arm underneath his and they left the garden.

*   *   *

Joseph Hedley was known throughout the territories and was well acquainted with its workings. A learned and accomplished man, he might be described as a do-gooder. Thom believed he could shed light on the confounded mystery. Even as he climbed the Minerva's steps to visit the Professor, he was clear in his head that he was on a trail important enough for his best effort.

He reached the door of Hedley's room, it was open a crack, like it was last time the sheriff came calling. He knocked, first softly, then harder. No answer.

"Professor?" the sheriff called out, "Professor Hedley, it's Thomas Powell." Still no answer. That was enough for the lawman to put his right hand on his pistol. With his other hand he gave the door a push. It opened wider. There was a sound coming from further in, from the second room in back. A low, repeating tone, creaking, strange.

Thom drew his pistol, held it up and out, and moved through the front. Everything was in place like he remembered: there was a chair with the round table set next to it, a shelf full of books of all shapes and subjects. A tired-looking settee ran along a wall. Then he reached the doorframe and looked inside the back room. A window was full open and a stiff breeze was blowing in.

Thomas was nothing less than ill when he saw. The professor's body was hanging by a rope from a beam in the rafter, there was a noose of thick hemp around his neck. A chair was kicked over on the floor beneath him. Wind was moving his body in a sad arch.

THE GODLESS MEN

BOOK TWO

Last Drop of Bad Blood

I

The Pawnee were an unusual people, even for Indians. Unlike other natives, including their mortal enemies the Sioux, they stayed put in a place. They were neither migrants nor nomads. When they settled into southeastern Nebraska generations ago, they took to making sod homes out of the surface soil of the green meadows that ran from water into rocky hills. Their crude but effective efforts made for strange-looking permanent settlements along branches of the Platte River. Traditional birch wood and deerskin wigwams were scattered among dwellings the shape of a child's building blocks.

The Pawnee were fierce but kept to themselves, cautiously venturing far afield only when it was necessary for hunting parties, tribal councils and such. White people recognized their standoffishness, were glad for it, and left them alone. They would not be left alone by the Sioux, who called themselves *Lakota*, which in their language means "the good friends." The two tribes hated each other, fought seasonally, but white people could hardly tell them apart. The Indians had bad blood between them for more years than the time of Europeans west of the Mississippi. Lakota and Pawnee made their land Indian Territory, union be damned.

Certainly, whites had their way. Nebraska joined the Union in '67, two years after the end of the terrible war. Folks in Nebraska went and changed the name of the town of Lancaster. It became "Lincoln," after the martyred President. The Burlington Railroad came hard charging following the hostilities. They laid iron throughout the state. It wasn't long before Lincoln was connected to Topeka easy as you please. More and more rail lines were planned.

After the army had chased natives away from white settlements, the Federal government took over the land and there was a lot of it. Feds gave it to railroads, insuring the land rights to lay their iron. As the great plan unfolded, there was land available for businessmen and common settlers. Free land also attracted schemers and deceivers and worse. Government did not much care who got parceled earth, long as it wasn't Indians.

There was partial peace in the state between settlers and natives. The Pawnee and Lakota stayed in Nebraska, roaming free enough in an expanse several days ride from Lincoln. The only settlement in a great stretch down there was called Wilber. The Indians could have killed those folks, though it would have been quite a shootout. But they weren't interested in Wilber; they were tired of fighting and losing. Natives just wanted to be left alone.

Nebraska was big enough for that, especially with Kansas and Missouri, hospitable places, as neighboring lands. The deal was if Indians could remain out of sight and control their urge to attack whites, they were allowed a semblance of their culture and way of life.

This is to say that a Pawnee settlement among the thick woods along the Platte River was a fine place for a man to hide. When David eased the Paint he stole onto a deer path outside the last trading post in Missouri, he took his sweet time entering Pawnee land. The deer path led to a river tributary easily passable. Trail picked up and widened after that, and led through forests of tall pines, oaks, and cedars, separated by wide fields of grass and bush. Hours into the journey, nary a soul to be seen, he was still cautious and ever alert. If he was found trespassing by Indians straight out, they might well kill a stranger as have a look.

Second day into the land he took to walking, partial as he was to walking through woods. He pulled his mount along slow, resting it and thus saving the horse for a hard ride if trouble came. He camped out under the stars; ate squirrel and wild cabbage leaves, drank creek water. Time in solitude was welcomed. He'd been in towns, talked to men too much. It was men and money that got him into his sad situation. McClure had killed whether he had a mind to or not. Now his desire was to lay down his gun and be left alone. Just like the Pawnee.

Evenings in Indian Territory he bedded at a tree line so he'd have some shelter but could still see the sky. The blond did not cotton to people, preferred to look into the heavens, compelled to watch blinking stars.

Feeling poorly he was. When he was in the Express, a boy, he'd ponder the future while on a long, easy ride. He would have good thoughts. Meet a gal, make money, there's a plan. Then war came, life changed. He volunteered for fighting like all his townspeople did, donning a shabby-looking grey uniform and a used pair of boots. He was not Davey anymore, rather Rebel with a firearm. He started out in Sikeston, becoming a member of a small army called the Fighting First. In that part of Missoura the land doglegs south. It closed in on Tennessee, so it was natural for McClure and his Sikeston boys to be sent there.

It didn't take long for the war to come. He got in scrapes even before the horror of Shiloh. He was a good soldier, always had been a crack shot, but there was more to his skill, he went about it the right way. Survival was natural, so was killing, he did not know why. Lots of his fellows were fighters, many were brave. He was smart and lucky too. When shooting started, he knew what to do to stay alive, all the while fighting like a true son of the South. He killed those who meant to kill him, fair enough. If one believed in the Devil, McClure's knack was a gift from hell.

*　　*　　*

One night sleeping in Pawnee land, he dreamed. Saw the beautiful redhead, clear as day. He was angry that he did not know her name. Dream made him twist up his blanket as he slept. How much decency would it take to know the name of the woman who was satisfying his needs and thought the world of him to boot? He was staring at the red hole in her face, one that could not hide her expression of surprise. Her death mask woke him up in a cold sweat. He blinked at the black sky. He got up, shook his head as if to dispel vapors and then took a cooling drink of water.

When he fell back asleep he dreamed about the Boss's man who sprung him from jail. In the dream Smith was taller than in real life, making him a giant. His undertaker's attire loomed like a monstrous ghost. The double-barreled shotgun became a slithering snake that attached itself to David and squeezed.

Blond woke in the dead of the night. The clear sky was a sparkling array of pins of light. He took a deep breath, got up and stood stretching, shaking off sleep. By and by he felt better, dreams don't mean a damn thing. It was the power of nature, shining strength down upon him. That's the way it always was with him, sounded like religion though it wasn't.

Next day, deeper in Pawnee land, was a cloudy, rainy one. He led his mount into a creek flowing from the Platte. The water was stirring and splashing with trout. David used the Paint to drive fish onto the shallows where he could club 'em. The horse did not mind stomping in the water and a couple trout were caught that way. He scaled, gutted, then cut the meat into pieces. He ate the fish raw, figuring he should not build a fire, inviting trouble. Any red man could spot the sorry-burning fire of a white man from miles away.

He bedded against a spreading oak whose branches grew wide enough apart to reveal the black and twinkling sky.

*   *   *

It was the third day or so. He walked the deer path, leading horse along. The deep woods were quiet. He did not care how long it took to get where he was going, wherever that might be. Strange feeling, like his life was over, ended back in town where Boy's life ended. Now he was biding time. He ate insects and blueberries that day, found a goodly-sized caterpillar and folded the bug around a broad leaf. It wasn't bad eating, given the circumstances.

He spent another night under the stars, glad to have the company of a horse. He missed Boy. There was something about that mount and David was truly sorry he was gone, as much as he'd ever felt for any man that was gone. That night Boy was in his dreams, running wild and free. David gave a whistle and he came. That horse had the biggest eyes. Now in the dream they galloped, easy as you please. Boy's eyes looked back at the rider, then the horse straightened his head toward the oncoming road. Damnedest thing, dreaming about an animal.

*   *   *

Next day, a fateful one, was a clear, warm day. He led his Paint into pine woods that were alive with the buzzing of insects and the chirping chatter of birds. As he and his horse passed through, the noise increased, like his presence was being announced by creatures of the thicket. He made his way easy enough through the tall pines. The terrain was passable without overmuch difficulty while the vegetation that abounded kept him hidden from view.

It was late-afternoon when he spotted them: two Pawnee braves, couple hundred yards into the hilly forest ahead. The natives were standing, staring, they spotted him back. He could make out their mounts further behind, un-tethered, as Indians never bother to tie their animals and never fear them wandering.

David approached, making no effort to conceal himself. He got within fifty yards, he gawked at the braves and they returned the favor. The braves looked alike, all Indians did. Both were shorter than he, but lean and muscled, their skin dark and their hair long and black. Neither was painted for war, likely just making their way through the woods hunting. Both carried army issue Springfield rifles, older models, but capable enough guns if Indians could shoot straight, which most could not. They also had bows slung across their backs and hatchets tucked at the waist-line.

The blond figured he could out-gun them, but that was not his intention. Instead, he let the rein of his mount go and strode up to the two. He got close and held his hand up in the traditional greeting of white man to red. His open palm rose up and down. The Indians returned the gesture. The Pawnee spoke in low voices, called out to McClure, but David spoke neither Pawnee nor any Indian tongue.

The white man reached real careful for his Bowie. He slide it out from its sheath, and showed it to the braves while he held his other hand out so as not to threaten. Damn, what a fine knife. It had a hand-carved bone handle and thick metal blade that glinted in sunlight. Any man would admire the weapon. The blond took the blade by the edge to throw it. He turned away from the two and tossed the knife at a tree near the braves but not close enough to be taken as an aggressive act. The Bowie flew through the bug-buzzing air and stuck a pine dead center, pretty as you please.

David had been told by a reliable fellow that Indians valued knives highly, would do anything for a good one, as they did not forge metals. He was now aiming to trade for friendship. The braves looked at the stuck knife, then at the one who threw it, then at each other. The blond motioned to the Indians to fetch it. One went over and pulled the blade out, held it, and made a face that the blond figured was an Indian smile. The second brave turned to the white man, who even now was removing his leather *chaparajos*. David tossed the leggings to the Indian, who caught them, showed off his take to the first brave. David didn't mind losing his chaps. He'd won 'em in a card game a while back, and they had served their purpose on long rides. With them off, his Confederate Grays were plain to see, the pants worse for wear. The faded red stripes of the Tennessee volunteers ran down from belt to cuff. The braves noticed the pants, said something to each other in Pawnee. Another thing that McClure had heard was that Indians favored Confederates. Rebels fought the same Union Blues that the Indians had been fighting.

Without another word or consideration, the braves took their booty and remounted their ponies. They sauntered away from the blond. One of them looked back and gave a wave to say "ain't you coming?" David got on his Paint and followed at a respectable distance.

THE GODLESS MEN

They traveled the rest of that day till it got dark and the pine woods gave way first to thin rows of cedars and white birch, then to grassland near the river. That's where the Pawnee settlement was, and in the distance David could see fires at campsites and a group of sod structures rising out of the ground. Made a strange sight, but he was glad to see it because he knew not many white men had. The braves passed one solitary sod block, not in the best condition, four sides of barely six feet. The thing was set away from the rest of the community. It was near water and sheltered by trees. The Indians stopped at it, looked back to the man who traded a fine knife and leather chaps. One of the braves gestured at the structure. David got the idea and stopped when he reached it. The braves continued to the main camp, giving no-never-mind. The blond hopped off his mount and led it to the sod home.

* * *

The place was a modest abode, a hut, not larger than the birch bough lean-tos he had fashioned during the war when Confederates ran out of tents. It smelled of moss and dung but was otherwise passable. Had a secure-enough thatch roof with a smoke hole. It was empty inside, so the blond unsaddled his mount, gathered his guns and gear, and moved in. As he did, he pondered why this one hut was set off from the community. Some kind of social outcast had lived here, or a leper, damn. It was humbling to live thus, destiny was having its way, and David was too shamed for pride.

He didn't venture those first few days. He lay real low. The nearby creek allowed him fresh water for drink and bathing. He did not want to draw attention by shooting, nonetheless he was able to kill a rabbit with his remaining Bowie. Took some throwing and missing but he got it done. He felt it safe enough to make a fire so he prepared a stew of skinned meat, scallion, pepper grass, and river water. Thus did he have a hot meal. Such a simple pleasure was welcomed, he ate the entire rabbit.

His horse was tethered at a stand of smoke trees that kept the mount in place yet gave it stomping space. It was happy enough feeding on grass, berries, and herbage. He had stolen an even-tempered animal. A good judge of animal flesh, he'd had a choice of two to steal, he considered each. One, a tan Morgan, was feisty, no sense taking a feisty animal into unchartered territory. This Paint he took was strong and willing, an easy choice. Wished he could tell men apart like that.

*   *   *

One morning David sat outside on the warming earth cross-legged like Indians do. He had a smoke and watched the village a short distance up river. There were squaws at water's edge, washing clothes and laying their things out on rocks to dry. They chatted amongst themselves. Nearby, young'uns ran and played, chasing each other among stout spruce. The blond could see braves stretching out a length of hide in the sun for tanning. In a patch of open field, several were breaking in new horses. It was the normal things folks do, red or white.

No one paid him much mind, he had to give Indians that. Private people they were, and minded their own affairs. Guess they believed McClure's enemies were no friends of theirs. The more he watched the tribe move about the village, he could discern individuals. He spotted one of the braves who traded with him, he waved at the Indian and the brave waved back. So at that time he concluded it wasn't true that all Indians look alike.

One bright sunny day he was practicing his knife throwing, striking trees from a good distance when his work caught the interest of two young Pawnee boys. They ventured over to watch, while nearby an older buck kept an eye out. The boys were shy but curious, and finally David motioned them over and showed them how he held the blade. They were real attentive. Then he reached back, threw, and hit a tree a good twenty yards away, dead center. The boys pointed, jumped about, and laughed, though McClure did not think knives were much funny. One of the young'uns tried to throw. He was no good and missed a nearby tree altogether and almost cut himself to boot. Second boy was better, his aim was true. His toss struck wood, but it was handle-first. The knife fell to the forest floor. Then the boys ran back to the still-watching buck. They chattered at the adult like children do, gesturing at the white man and retelling their adventure with knife throwing. David wiped his blade on tattered Reb pants and went back to his lodging.

*　　　*　　　*

It was a moonless night and a blazing fire at the settlement and the voices of the Pawnee caught his attention and brought him out of his abode. Other quiet evenings there were small fires spread out among the sod homes and wigwams. It was like this was a special occasion, a gathering of clans, and the blond got curious. He made his way quiet-like to get closer to the proceedings. He knew Indians had a reputation for stealth. Common knowledge they could sneak upon a wagon train or campfire of whites easy as they pleased. Not to take away from them, but he was skilled himself, having done his share of hunting before the war and scouting during it. One time in Georgia he crawled on his belly for a quarter mile to spot Union artillery, went past sentries like he was a ghost under a waning moon. When it came to craftiness, *he* was the native.

Quiet steps, sure steps were used to approach. He got on his belly for a stretch forward, then he crouched, moving tree to tree. There was a thick stand of oaks and underbrush not twenty yards from the blaze. He got there. There was a goodly number of Indians in the firelight. The blond sat on the cool earth and watched through the tree branches. There were men, women, and children, like the entire tribe had been summoned. Half dozen or so elders were in charge. There was scattered conversing among the people. Babies were crying in their mother's arms. Natives were chanting, as if to call upon spirits; tom-toms were beating. All the while the great fire sent burning embers and popping pinecones into the night sky. For a country boy from Kirksville, never knowing Indians close up, it was a most-strange sight. Why were the clans gathered?

Off to one side of the great fire, illuminated by the blaze, the Pawnee had lashed logs of pines with river reed, thus fashioning one of their toting boards to drag supplies and possessions. Three carcasses of buffalo lay on the pine logs. David figured they had been dragged from the prairie after a hunt. The buffalo were not of great size, in fact they appeared scrawny, though the blond was no judge of bison. Scuttlebutt had it one of the animals could weigh one thousand pounds. By any measure the dead creatures on the pine logs were barely five hundred combined.

There were Indian braves and their women sitting cross-legged around the palette of carcasses. Drumming stopped and it got quiet. The elders in feathered headdresses spoke to each other in rising voices and also to Indians gathered, who were talking back to them and each other. Braves gestured at the buffalo, then held their hands up to heaven and shook them. One elder got up and knelt at the lashed pine logs. Man appeared tormented, arms out, gazing into the black sky. Blond saw a squaw and her child, near the elder. Whatever words were being said were sad as the woman was crying and holding her child tight.

McClure was mystified by the proceedings. He ventured a guess that it was concerning a bad hunt, three scrawny animals for the entire tribe. In that case, times would be hard, children would go hungry. He did not pretend to understand the ways of these red men. He left the gathering at the bonfire, and went back to his sod place, as quiet as he came.

*   *   *

Solitude gave him time to reflect, not a welcomed activity. He pondered his deeds, he did not care for the man he was. Here was no thinker or dweller on that already done, so the contemplating was more like a bug inside his ear, one that would not stop buzzing.

98

THE GODLESS MEN

One night his solitude ended. He was surprised to hear approaching footsteps outside. He knew it was an Indian in moccasins, the tread was measured and quiet. Someone stood at his doorway, then parted the hide-flap and entered the sod shelter.

It was a squaw from the village. She was a fit, black-haired young woman, a hard worker judging from her rough, dark hands, and stern, tanned countenance. David was on the ground cleaning his rifle when she entered. She said something softly in her language and motioned with her hands back to the village. She spoke again pointing at him. She wore the faintest smile.

He did not know what she could be saying or what the matter was until she stepped into the small fire's light. The woman had a scar across the side of her face. Thing ran down her cheek in a crooked line. Looked to have been cut a while ago. It meant she had been marked by her people as a female taken by a white man or one who had given herself. Either way, no brave would have her. She sat down across from him, said nothing. She mostly looked at the earth and moved her fingers in the dust, like she was painting a picture though she wasn't. He paid her little mind while he finished his work. She pointed at his rifle and said words that he figured were Pawnee for "gun."

When it was time for sleep, he put out the fire and turned in. He figured she'd come, she did, lifting the deerskin blanket and sliding next to him. He was on his back, neither spoke 'cept the language of bodies. He had never been with a squaw. She was a dusty girl and did not smell of perfume like his former. Still, she was soft to the touch and he was a man. She was astride 'im.

*   *   *

The outlaw knew he could not live in sod for the rest of his days. He'd killed men, even lawmen, now posses crisscrossed the land. Law neither forgives nor forgets, if the hunt takes time, justice has time. Many lawmen and bounty hunters live to hunt outlaws and kill them. After the dark deeds the blond done, those coming would have a good length of rope to hang him, judge and jury be damned. Pawnee territory was a good ways from where white men roam. Every day with Indians was a day of not hanging. Still, it was no life for his kind.

He had a thought to make his way to Canada, still a good stretch north, but he could not abide cold. He had a fancy to venture to Beaver Falls, just inside Nebraska from the Missouri border. It was a piddling town with miners who worked the nearby hills for metals. He could get lodging, a job, a woman, he had greenbacks. Trouble was the blond could not dig dirt for a living to cover his hiding, could never enter the dark of a mine and descend into the earth. No sun or moon nor stars. That was ungodly, he was not cut from that cloth.

The past just would not lift, fade, and disappear like morning mist from the peach fields of Shiloh. More than a fortnight after he arrived among the Pawnee, he had a troubling feeling. One evening as he sat outside at the bank of the river with the squaw, he saw a faint, flickering light across the Platte. He would have sworn he smelled white man which was strange him being one. Maybe since he had the squaw he was different. He looked again into the dark and there was no light. Must be imagination.

Next day, under a bright sun, he mounted his Paint and ventured across the Platte along pebbly shallows. Sure enough he picked up the trail of a single rider with a shod mount. Indians don't shoe animals, he knew it was a white. Later he found a campsite that had been covered up good but was there. David guessed it was a bounty hunter, one trying to scare up business by nosing around Indians, judging any man he came upon would likely be wanted. The blond was thinking the fellow was a capable gun, but took a chance riding a shod animal in Pawnee land.

That night, David tethered his mount a distance from a low burning campsite, eased his way toward it. He crouched in shadows and watched an older gent poke a stick of squirrel into a fire. He was tough-looking, sure enough a southerner. He wore an old red hat, with the front brim pulled way up. Just like that, the blond emerged from brush and strode up to the campsite.

Further beyond a horse neighed, which would be the man's mount tied at the short oaks.

"Stranger," is what the blond stated. Startled, the man dropped his stick full of squirrel into the fire.

"Stranger," the old-timer answered. The two stared, one standing, one sitting. The blond held a hand on his Colt. The man cast a glance at the yellow-boy leaned against a tree some feet from reach. Whoosh, David drew pistol from leather. The man's eyes got real large and afeared. Truth was David did not want to kill if it was possible not to.

"This is Pawnee land," the blond said.

The sitting man got up real slow, with his hands out wide to show he was unarmed. He was brave, straightening up tall before he spoke. "I might say the same to you."

"I'm thinking you're a bounty hunter."

The man grunted. He understood his dire straits and looked at David serious. "That's only a concern if you're a wanted man," he said.

"You trailing any particular fellow?"

The old-timer thought about it, there was no sense pretending. "I am," he said.

"Who might it be?"

"Name of David McClure."

"He a wanted man?"

"Next to the James and Younger boys, he's the one."

"What did he do so bad?"

"Murdered folks for no good reason, killed a beloved sheriff and deputy in St. Joe, I heard he killed his own horse." The gent spoke in a breath, like it was exciting. It got quiet, gun still pointed. Nearby, the man's horse snorted like wondering if its master was okay.

There was a time McClure might have kilt at a threat. "Where did you serve?" he asked of him under his gun.

"Georgia, defended Atlanta, fought that bastard Sherman all the way to the sea."

"Hot in Georgia."

"Got fire ants crawl inside holes in your shoes and bite, hurts like hell, you scratch until you bleed. How about you?"

"From Missoura, fought thereabouts."

"First thing I noticed was your Reb pants. I'll tell you, worst thing ever happened since God's creation was Abraham Lincoln."

"Shouldn't talk like that, you're in a union state."

"Union go to hell, this is Indian land."

David would have laughed, if he was the sort. Instead, he holstered his pistol. "Have to let you live."

The man let out a breath, then took one. "You McClure?" he asked.

"I'm the man who is not going to shoot you." The old gent nodded gravely, as if a fair deal had been struck. "I'm obliged," he said.

The blond picked up the yellow-boy from the tree. He pumped the lever, removing three cartridges. He looked the gun over, not a bad weapon, then returned it to its leaning position.

"Have to steal your horse though," David said.

*   *   *

He took the man's mount, a fine enough animal. With it in tow, he crossed back over the Platte, returning to the tribe's settlement. Next day he traded the horse to the Pawnee for a sack of dried *maize* and deerskin pants and shirt. He got the worse of the deal but it was no matter. The corn would last a while. Far as the deerskins, he was truly tired of wearing secession garb. Colors told too much.

His last night at the hut was a starry cool evening with a waxing moon. He sat outside with the squaw, they both stared at the twinkling sky. He reached out and held her hand in his, gave hers a squeeze, close as he could come to thanking her. She smiled back and kissed his hand. They returned to the hut and he had her a last time. He had gotten used to coupling. Afterwards, he stole glances as she lay asleep next to him. She'd been the quiet type these weeks. She spent her days at the river, washing or fishing. One time she caught a trout, made him a fine repast. She'd speak with a few squaws who had not disowned her, the group giggled at some talk or gossip like women do. She would laugh with the others and David felt good that she was happy enough with her state. Who was she, how did she get that scar, did she have any kin among the tribe? He pondered but could not communicate and thus would never know much about her.

Day he left, he sent her off in the morning while he broke camp. He had to motion and speak sternly to get her to understand he was leaving for good. She was sad to see him go and cried tears. So in turn he acted kindly. As he departed, they waved to each other like friends. She called out in Pawnee, he figured her words were akin to "fare thee well." He allowed himself the notion that he would return someday. Never did know her name, same exact thing with the redhead.

So on a cloudy day he led his Paint away from the settlement, following a narrow path along a branch of water. He knew that the bounty hunter would find his way to civilization and tell the law that McClure was among the Pawnee. That would make folks curious. They would arrive and they would have guns.

Though he left the Indians, it wasn't like he cared if he lived or died, he was resigned to fate but nonetheless would not wait for the vengeful God to find him. He did not want to hang by his neck in public nor die in a bloody shootout with the Law. Weird, he was ready to die, just not like that.

The outlaw pondered. If he was to live one day to the next, it was wrong-headed running away from men. A better way to hide was among them. That's when he rode southeast to Topeka.

II

Thomas was hardly one to contemplate matters of love. While stoically at ease on the battlefield, emotional turmoil was a foreign land where didn't have a map, nor did he speak the language.

He was with Baili in a park on Delaware Lane. They sat on an oaken bench in a gazebo, both quietly contented. Around them were sounds of the evening. There was wind in trees and cricket chirps, lightning bugs were about. A light rain began to fall with a soft hissing. The shower would have a cooling effect on a late-summer day.

After some thought, he understood something about his own feelings and the understanding made him afeared. He spoke to Baili: "You told me when we first met that you would return someday to your home, to China."

She did not look at him. "Yes," she answered. She moved her hands in her lap then held one upon the other. His was a serious tone she knew, and the tender thoughts between them were real.

"I was a girl when I came, so young they mistake me for a boy. When my father died I told myself I must return one day, my duty to my family." As she spoke, she tugged at the bottom of her dark-green waistcoat.

Her struggle to express herself in English had a touching effect, he simply listened and considered. Words are powerful, both were afraid of them. What comes next in conversing and what would the consequences be? Thomas felt desperation, an odious temperament.

He stated in one breath: "I want to be with you and I want you to be with me." No further words, those described the baffling currents that swept him. She considered what he had said, making sure she heard correctly.

"That cannot be," she said in a voice as to be barely heard. Rain picked up and pinged upon the roof of the gazebo. "You are white," she concluded albeit sadly. He did not pretend to not understand. Indians run off, Chinese good for railroad labor, black folks lost in the midst. Whites moved about pretty as you please. Guess that was fair enough, after all, it was their country.

His words came slow but sure. "If you can't be with me because of the man I am, or because danger abounds, those are reasons," he said in a lightly trembling voice, "Our color is not a reason, not if we care about each other."

Her eyes were cast out into the rain, right flustered. Taking a good breath, she settled down, you could see her thinking. Gathering words as in a field of wildflowers, picking this one, not that one.

She finally spoke in a soft and strong voice. "I want to be with you." They kissed modestly, a dear thing. Her cheeks reddened when they separated, darned if his didn't too. Holding hands, Thomas and Baili sat contented surrounded by forsythia. Drops of water hit the wooden rail, making a tap tapping sound.

*　　　*　　　*

Thomas was in his room at the Porter Hotel having a smoke. Seated in a sturdy wooden chair leaned back against a wall, a precarious post, he looked down on busy Vermont. As he puffed a briar-wood pipe, white whiskers of smoke escaped out the window.

He pondered the war. Seemed he did that regular, natural enough. Any man who fought would possess memories and be haunted by them.

He thought on Chickamauga. It would have been September of '63, in Georgia. It was that battle where he came close to getting himself killed. The union commander, an honest but incapable General name of Rosecrans, had not wanted to fight. As a result, he deployed his divisions in a lackluster manner. He was outnumbered by the Confederate General Braxton Bragg and toward the end of the first day of fighting the Grays had turned union flanks on two sides. Thomas, now at the rank of sergeant, found himself and his fellows in dire straits with Grays coming from three directions.

He was in the midst of artillery fire from twelve-pound cannons, anyone who has not experienced such a thing can never know how frightening it unfolds. The air was roaring with the sounds of discharge and the earth was shaking mightily. Solid shot and shrapnel were hitting men in myriad ways, tearing flesh and entire limbs, summoning angels in heaven. His Major, a brave and decent man name of Boucher, had his head taken clean off. Seeing the beating that blues were taking, half the entire Kansan unit up and ran, following the lead of Rosecrans himself, who retreated from the field at the height of the proceedings.

Sergeant Powell was able to form a line of fire with some boys in blue. They got themselves behind a low stone wall at a branch of Chickamauga creek. Nearby were union artillery pieces manned by Ohioans. For sure the Federals were hard pressed by lines of approaching Gray.

At the crest of a hill directly behind his position he spotted his division commander, General George Henry Thomas, who had declined to withdraw from the battle. General Thomas had himself a row of artillery and two score of riflemen and they were trying their damnedest to address the breaches in the union line.

The Sergeant, who wasn't a man to holler, could not help but urge his fellows: "Stiffen up, boys, there's General Thomas, standing tall!"

Between artillery and the directed fire of Winchesters, the union's line tightened. Bloody fighting followed but Grays were now getting as good as they gave. The General's stubborn bravery was plain to see and a battle that could have been a rout and disaster for the Union turned into a stalemate.

General Thomas was thereafter known as "Rock of Chickamauga," a right proper moniker.

*   *   *

Reverie over, he was clear on what his duty as town officer of Lawrence was. Can't dodge a righteous fight. He took his pipe and struck the contents into a clay bowl set on the window ledge.

He then left the Porter and made his way to the Minerva, the unfortunate Professor's abode.

In the lobby he found a bushy-haired Scotsman, McMurphy, working the front desk like he did most days since the place opened. The lobby of the hotel was empty and quiet, suiting the sheriff. He strode in and the man put down the paper he was reading. Wind came and the paper's pages fluttered.

"Evening," Thom said.

"Sheriff Powell, good evening, what brings you here?"

Thomas had a notion and wasn't one to dance about it. "Mr. McMurphy, you related that you were behind this desk the night Hedley was killed, and that you didn't see nor hear a thing out of the ordinary."

Sheriff spoke in a tone that gave the man pause. He could not hold the lawman's gaze. "That is correct, strange I know but that's the way it was."

"It is strange. I spoke with a fellow who strolled by that night and said you were not here." Nothing more to be added. McMurphy opened his mouth but did not speak. There was no such witness. Any card player knows the worth of a bluff. The Scotsman, redder-faced than usual, commenced to stammering.

"What I said was that while I was behind this desk I saw no one come by, that's the Lord's truth." The man smiled like he was satisfied with his words. So he made a poor joke: "I mean if a man has to pee he has to pee."

Before any further utterances, Thom reached out both hands and took McMurphy by his shirt and pulled him face to face. With the counter top between the two, the man was off his feet, a fish on a hook. Sheriff took his time speaking. "Sir, one thing I do well, spot a lie. Lies have a way."

Now the man did not know what to make of this show of force and emotion, he was perspiring like a yard-hand. "I wouldn't lie to you, you're a gentleman," he pleaded unconvincingly.

With that Thom released his grip with a push back. McMurphy left this shirt rumpled, showing finger marks on the fabric. The lawman wasn't finished by a measure. He held a hand on the butt of his pistol and lowered his voice.

"I will tell you a dark secret of mine. I've killed more than any outlaw, I do not intend to but it happens. Regards this dastardly murder, I will kill the next man who crosses me."

Quite a display, more than sufficient. McMurphy took a deep breath, got calm-faced, and spoke. "I stepped away, wasn't to pee," he began in a croak like a frog. "A snarly-type came in around eight that evening, said I could use some air, told me to skedaddle. I was afeared of him, he was a serious man. When I came back, the lobby was empty. Don't know a thing else."

It had the ring of truth. Lawman took his hand off his gun, and removed from his vest pocket the wanted poster of McClure. The paper was not a canny likeness, but good enough.

"Was this the snarly type?" McMurphy looked at the sheriff, then at the piece of paper, then back. He shook his head no. "Man that night was older and darker, had a moustache."

Thomas had a feeling, one he would not shy from. Staring cold, he folded the poster into his pocket and gave his Spiller a push into the leather. He turned his back to the man and left.

*　　　*　　　*

There was one E.J. Muller, a man of reputation in the territories. A medical doctor of distinction during the war, he served the union over in Shenandoah Valley. In the matter of the hanged professor, he had been sent by the state government to Lawrence. Muller was a quiet, calculating sort, wore bifocal spectacles. He was certainly a gentleman, but a slow worker. Here was no crack investigator. He had examined Hedley's body before it was interred, he concluded yes the man had been hanged. He had examined the scene of the crime and posited that the killer hid in the back room, waited in ambush and struck the poor man with a cudgel, rendering him helpless. E.J. sent reports to Topeka, and telegrams were sent back. The doctor seemed well satisfied in the job he was doing, so seemed Topeka. In fact Marshal Quinn came to Lawrence, turned out he was friends with the good doctor.

Consensus posited McClure finished the spree he started. Sheriff did not fancy that theory, made no common sense. Rather he thought that Muller was too casual an investigator. Hedley deserved better.

So Powell sought out the doctor, finding the man in a courtyard outside his office, enjoying a chew. Muller had just spit a good distance, hitting a lamppost. He was surprised to spot a visitor. Thom strode with purpose, stopped right at where the man was standing.

"Mr. Muller."

"Sheriff," came a mumble.

"I want to speak to you about this terrible crime."

Doctor seemed well prepared as to what to say. "Shocking as it was," he began with a long face, "I was determined to come to your aid. So urgent was my cause, I rode a horse to here, frankly, my posterior hurt for a week."

Thom cut the blather short. "Was the man right or left handed?" he inquired.

Muller's eyes widened at the question. "Who's that, the murderer?"

"Him."

"Right or left, how could I know that?"

Powell got red some, shrugged. He was getting annoyed. "Sir, you're an investigator, educated man, a public servant."

"Public servant?" E.J. was offended, servant indeed, but he was also intimidated. "Right or left, the poor man was hanged. Died of asphyxiation, that's the medical fact." He sniffed, putting his glasses back on.

Took effort to be patient, the sheriff expended the effort. "Think about it, if a left-hander hanged a man, he'd place the rope different than if he was right handed."

Muller twisted his face, Thom could not tell if he was acting or not. If he was acting dumb, he was a good actor.

Sheriff got menacing: "Had I a rope, I'd demonstrate, place it around your neck. I'm a righty." Thomas never talked thusly to folks. His tone and physical presence spoke of impending doom. E.J. saw the light. He cleared his throat, stood up straight, and assumed a professional tone.

"Sheriff Powell, I see. I see now what you're getting at. A right-handed man would loop a rope around from the right, a left-hander opposite. That would bring the knot to one side or the other slightly, accordingly, yes. The resultant bruises on skin would verify the positioning." That was more positing than Muller had done his entire stay in Lawrence. He touched his own neck, rubbed the skin. He continued: "If that is the case, then Professor Hedley was hanged by a left-handed man. As you pointed out, I am a state investigator, my considered opinion would be left hander."

Such nervous testimony was hardly convincing, still Thomas gave him his due. He did not push further. In return the man was happy to be saving face.

The sheriff was not done. "One more thing. Have you come across a dark, mustached fellow?"

More theatrics from Muller. "I do not recall such a person, many sport facial hair," he offered with an expression betraying his intentions. Thomas tipped his hat and departed the yard.

*   *   *

It was Saturday evening, Sheriff in his office, routines of evenings past. He had relieved Farnsworth who had obligations at home. Thom had no such thing. All he had was the wanting to be anywhere else.

All three jail cells were occupied. At the end was a cowhand from a cattle drive out of West Tennessee who'd showed a hot temper in a saloon fight. Second guest was a man named Sims who was a familiar face, Lawrence's town drunk. Man up front near the sheriff's desk was a thief who gave his name as Rogers. He was a quiet type determined to take his punishment. The three were settled in, had gotten corn meal and beans, and were happy enough considering their no-account state. So Thom sat back and pondered.

What he desired was to court his gal like other folks court. But he could not as long as there was peril. Much as he'd like to toss his tin badge and leave the territory with Baili in tow, he never would without first attending to unfinished business.

*   *   *

DeCamp arrived by train from St. Joe that evening. Thomas had asked for his help, needing to know what a newspaperman could find. None better for the job, here was a hard case and a trusted friend. The two sat at the sheriff's desk late into the night, disturbed only by the snoring of prisoners. Ben read notes he had made. He was real earnest, just as he had been as a soldier in war.

"I spoke with the widow of Basil Early, she confirmed his intention to open a college for Indians on land outside of Maryville."

Thom was surprised. "College for Indians," he had to shake his head at the thought, "not many would cotton to such a thing."

"Early was a Missourian and pro-union. Seems he had it in his mind to help the native people of the land."

"There's a high minded notion," Powell opined.

"Then there was Hedley," Ben spoke in measured tones, knowing the professor had been Thom's friend.

"A good man," the sheriff confirmed.

"Not sure where he comes into play."

"Curious, Hedley was a man to see the Indians side."

DeCamp studied his notes. "Not sure if it means anything but the Professor may have known Richard Stoddert."

That fact gave Thomas a start. "Stoddert, the fellow shot in Seneca?"

"On the 4th of July, the same. Hedley also attended King Edward College in Delaware, both wrote for the college's newspaper."

Powell did not respond, well in thought, like carrying a burden. DeCamp sensed his friend's mood. "Thomas, you need not take this upon yourself. The man to dispense justice is the

Territorial Marshal, he's got plenty of help, a passel of bucks who like to fight."

Thomas got up from his desk, took out a smoke. Connor Quinn was no dispenser of justice. He and his boys were overly interested in hanging McClure. These thoughts he did not want to share, it was more than his friend needed to know.

"The Marshal's busy chasing the James Boys," is what the sheriff said.

* * *

Storm was raging in Lawrence, howling wind blowing sheets of rain. Not proper weather for anything 'cept hunkering down. Thomas was in his office, staring at drops of water that fell from a leak in the roof and attempted to land in a tin bucket. The bucket was small, making certain that water was missing and falling astray. There was now a sizable puddle on the jail floor. He did not care to mop.

It was not supposed to be his shift, but the foul weather meant his deputy could not leave his homestead. Only the thief Rodgers remained imprisoned, he was suitable company. When he was not sleeping, he kept to himself, as silent a prisoner as any jailer could want. The sheriff listened to the buffeting storm and the dripping within. He was feeling blue, damn the notion, he loathed self-pity.

He pondered the war. He thought about a likeable man name of Abel, last name now forgotten. Knew the fellow at Chickamauga. Thom was with him in a flat, wide field early in the battle. The blues had been advancing until Gray firepower stopped the advance with iron and lead. The artillery fire of crushing shot had quieted, leaving behind the moans of pained wounded and the deafening silence of the dead. That was when Corporal Powell noticed Abel. He was hit, hurt bad, flat on his back blinking into gathering twilight.

"Lord preserve me," he said in a whisper. Thomas barely heard the lament, until it was repeated, "Lord preserve me," and then said again, like a holy man chanting. Abel died right there on the field, his hands clasped in prayer.

The image of Abel was powerful, though prayer was foreign to Thomas. Seemed futility to implore deliverance in war. The die had been cast by then.

Sheriff's reverie was broken. There was a knock on the door, slightest rap. He fancied he recognized the tapping. Thom answered and there she was. Baili's parasol had been hard pressed to keep her dry in arriving, barely succeeding. Thomas smiled at the sight of her.

"Please, come in," was all he could say.

Her face was wet with rainwater and just then a drop ran from her eye down her cheek and to her mouth. His eyes followed the arc of water.

She was pleased to be there, weather notwithstanding. "I went to the hotel, they told me you were working," she stated.

"Gosh you're wet."

"No problem, it is raining only water."

Thom took her parasol and soaked overcoat and directed her to a dry corner of the room. He tossed another log into the pot belly stove. She looked at the bucket and spreading spilt water, smiled at the sheriff.

"I can mop that for you," she offered. Thom gave a wave like no-such-thing. Baili was holding a willow wicker basket with a cloth laid over the top.

"What do you have there?" he inquired. There was the unmistakable smell of a square meal.

"Good food," she said simply and presented the basket, removing the linen cloth and lifting the lid. It was a feast of chicken and biscuits, best thing he had seen in a spell, excepting she who brought it.

"I prepared fried kitchen," Baili said and made a face, and said the word kitchen again. She got flustered, realizing she had the wrong word. Thomas was kindly amused.

113

"Wait, in the kitchen you cook," she offered. She tapped her head with an open hand. "Fried chicken," he pronounced and they both had a laugh.

She was proud of the repast. "Miss Dorothy showed me how," she explained. Baili was dressed in a long, tan smock over a dress the color of heaven. Without the slightest immodesty, she brought light and warmth into the damp room.

*   *   *

The two ate fried kitchen, speaking of this and that, the weather, the boarding house. Then came a spell of silence save the rain that fell outside. There was something behind the quiet, a portent. He felt it like an omen of dread. Thom did not want to spoil this happy occasion.

Still he had to tell her. "I have to go away and it's going to be dangerous," he said. She nodded like she understood though he knew she didn't.

"Can I come with you?" she asked. The innocence of the question brought a welling of tears. He shed tears when his mom died, though he did not during the worst of the war. Baili's query was powerful, he held her hands in his.

"It's not possible for you to come," he said.

She looked down at the jailhouse floor, then up at him. "It is easy to die."

He did not know why she would say that. "Yes," he answered.

"I wish I could help you."

"You do."

"How do I help you?"

He did not rightly feel at ease, still he had to speak his mind. He discovered words as he went along. "You are the most unique girl. How can I ever meet your extraordinary kind again? I do not want to leave you, but I am duty bound."

She bowed her head, there were tears in her eyes. The emotion was not self-pity, but defiance. She wiped the tears away like she didn't want them. Then she blinked up at Thomas.

114

"If I cannot come with you then do what you must do and come back."

They were close, he held her. "There are men who kill to get their way," he offered. She raised her head. "Kill them first," she stated. No more words. The wind rattled the windows.

*   *   *

Baili departed as late as she could and still get back to the boarding house before the front door was closed and locked. They had chatted a good spell, easy talk. She told him of the *Qing*, a great dynasty in China that had ruled her country for centuries. The rulers were foreigners, *Manchu*. Those folks were strict administrators, which did China good. As for Baili herself, she was born in Xiamen, a coastal city. It was from there she and her father braved the perilous sea passage to California. Xiamen was one of the treaty ports after the Opium War of 1842. That was when the first western missionaries appeared. She met one named John, from the country of England, older man with kind eyes. He taught her words of English, turned out she had an affinity for the strange language.

When it was time for her to depart that night, Thomas could not leave his post to accompany her. He flagged down an employee at the general store and the man brought a buckboard around. Right there in front of the driver of the conveyance, Thomas kissed Baili. He offered a helping hand as she stepped up into her seat.

*   *   *

When he went back inside the office, the thief Rodgers was up in his cell. Outside the rain lessened. Thom poured himself coffee at the stove, saw that his prisoner was watching. He held a cup up to him in an offer and the man nodded, so the sheriff brought thick, brown drink to the bars.

"Obliged," the man said.

Thomas sat back at his desk, content to listen to the rain. But he sensed the thief had something on his mind, so the lawman half turned until the two faced each other.

115

"She's a China-woman," Rogers said. Sheriff did not reply. The prisoner continued: "I don't mean nothing, just saying."

Sheriff could have found offense if he was the sort. "She's Chinese," the lawman corrected. The thief took a step closer and held the cell's bar with one hand while he sipped his coffee with the other.

"Chinese," he repeated. "I'm from California way, lots of 'em there."

"Californian, are you?"

"Sir, born in Santa Barbara, though have not been in many-a-year. You ever make it to Californ-i-ay?"

"I have, Chinese *men* there."

"What brought you out to the far west?"

"I was a boy."

"You don't strike me like a gold seeking 49er. Desperate men, those. Hope that don't describe your pa."

"It does not. I rode the Pony Express."

The prisoner slapped his leg. "A mail rider, I knew it. Me, I couldn't do that work as horses do not seem to like me."

"They say horses are good judges of character."

"I have heard that."

"You hate work altogether, I'd venture a guess."

"Sheriff, I am a thief, but I am not lazy."

"Folks would say for sure a thief is lazy, would rather steal than work."

"Sadly, I have been unlucky." The man laughed like he felt good. He lifted his cup at the lawman. "You may be a jailer, but you're ok."

"We will see how you feel tomorrow, when I bind your hands and send you off on the train to Topeka."

"No never mind, I know Topeka well."

"Have you met Marshal Quinn?"

"Have seen 'im, I have not met 'im and hope not to."

"He's the law there, you *will* be meeting him."

116

Rogers thought about it, shrugged. "That is my sad fate. We will see by and by." He placed his empty cup outside the bars onto a spindly table. He slapped at his side again, something Thomas guessed was a nervous tic. The prisoner sat on his bunk. Seemed to be talking to himself, though he wasn't.

"Makes me imagine what a small country this here union is becoming, know what I mean, Sheriff?"

"How's that?"

"The war brought folks together, didn't it? Missourians and Kansans live in proximity, like it or not. A Chinese woman in Lawrence, fancy that. What this union has done! I take you for a Yank, I can tell you were a fine soldier, I admire the kind because I was not."

Thom figured his prisoner a queer sort with schooling but without proper guidance or experience. Turned out schooling was wasted. Here was a thief, a common unfortunate, dishonest fellow, yet full of opinions.

The sheriff judged no harm in conversing. "In the way you say, the fighting did bring togetherness," he confirmed, thinking of Baili. The thief nodded like he understood though he did not. There was silence as a sharp wind blew and shook the room in a mild tremor. Then Rogers spoke: "Like me coming upon that quick stop fellow, soldier and mail-carrier."

Thom stopped at the words. A feeling rushed cold, the kind gives men pause. He turned away a tad, then looked at Rogers. Prisoner was flat on his back, staring at roof beams. The lawman stepped to the cell.

"Quick Stop," Thom stated.

"Yeah," Rogers grunted.

"Tall blond pony rider."

"He claimed to be a rider, I believed him. We was in the war for sure. Quiet sort, and a hellish fighter."

"Serve the confederacy, did you?"

"Deserter, if you must know. I stuck around Tennessee for a while. I am not a coward, rather a realist."

More blather from the prisoner, Thom wanted him back on track. "Guess you know how that fellow got the appellation Quick Stop."

"The man was a hell of a shot, could shoot buttons off shoddy coats."

Thom spoke casual-like. "So he's in Topeka."

Rogers was struck by the comment. He got up slow from his bunk, wearing a smirk on his face. "Sheriff, you got curious fast, is Johnny Reb a friend?"

"Name just sounds passing familiar," came the lie.

Rogers was not convinced. "I have to tell that I do believe in honor among thieves and can say no more." The prisoner had guessed that they were conversing about a wanted man. Rodgers was finished talking. The lawman shrugged like it didn't mean a thing. He turned down the lamp light.

III

Topeka means "place to find potatoes" in the Lakota language. Strange name, stood to reason that there would be potatoes aplenty in Topeka. There were not. Folks figured that it was Indians making fun in a way no white understood. Regardless, that was the appellation from time immemorial and so it stuck.

Like any place in the new land, Topeka started out small. A settlement developed because it was a suitable place to cross the Kansas River. The famed Oregon Trial began nearby and in the early 1800s wagon trains headed west from staging points to the green valleys of Oregon Territory. Then came 1861 and the momentous day Jayhawkers joined the Union as the 34th state. By year 1868 Topeka had seen considerable growth and was the capital city of Kansas. Work commenced on a grand state building, modeled after the Federal Capitol back east, there were sundry architects at it. By all accounts, the former outpost along the river was destined for expansion and prosperity.

Such facts meant nuthin' to McClure. He had never been in Topeka, couldn't care a hoot for history, it was a place to lose himself. Wasn't hard, easier than he thought it would be. He approached the town on a stormy day from the southwest, through passable woods of oaks and maples, following an old deer and Indian trail, the poor side. Where the way turned into a proper road, he came upon a grouping of weatherworn, pine-shingle buildings. One had a corral with a wide yard of turned-up dirt and manure, fenced a good amount of horses, judging from appearance. As David rode up he saw stalls inside and he could hear the animals fussing and snorting. The blond eased up on his Paint, stopped.

The only other being out there that day was a grizzled-faced geezer with a wild head of white hair. He was sitting on a bale of harvest grass, chewing on a twig. Man got up as the rider hopped off his mount.

"Morning, you run this place?" David inquired.

"That I do, own it, run it, such as it is," was the answer. Straight out the blond said he was looking for honest work.

"So, Stranger, you know horses?" the man asked. He was short and craggily, plain none too good to look at. No matter, the blond had practiced what to say.

"I know how to ride, walk 'em, and tend. I'm a devout Christian, a hard worker and honest."

"Uh-huh."

"I fought for this great Union, God Bless Abraham Lincoln; all I need is a loft to lay in and a job to do."

"Union army, eh?"

"Sir, fought at Shiloh, drove the Grays from the Hornet's Nest time and again 'til the end."

"Hornet's Nest, I am surprised to meet a survivor of that scrape."

"Survivor, sometimes I wish I weren't," he said real solemn. McClure shuffled his feet and looked down into the corral's dust. This boy could have been an actor. He had figured right that the old man was a Unionist. The owner raised his dark eyebrows and got a funny look, like he might cry.

"Stranger, out here in the hinterland we don't get patriotic veterans," the man began. "If it's a fresh start you're after, you have one."

"I'm obliged to you."

"What's your name?"

"Name's Haddix, out of Oakridge, Kentucky."

"Earl's my name."

"Pleasure to make your acquaintance."

"What brings you to Kansas?"

More acting: "My folks passed away back in Kentuck, stomach affliction. I have been heading west, relying on the Lord's mercy and hoping for the same."

The two shook hands hard. "Alright, son, welcome to Topeka."

*   *   *

Thus did McClure have a place to bed and a day's work to do. Earl proceeded to show David around. Job paid fifty cents a week in addition to beans, bread, and coffee. The corral was comprised of two sizeable shacks set aside the other. There was a commode at an outcropping of smoke trees and shrub pines. Earl lived in a cabin of roughly hewed oak logs with a thick thatch roof. One building of the corral contained stables, ten in all. There was a storage loft above. David bunked in the loft. There was good-enough bedding; a small table and chair set up for eating, smoking, and such. There was an open window with a shutter swung out; from there the approach road could be seen. That made David feel safe. Excepting for a lack of heat, unless he went down to the yard where an iron barrel was set for starting fire, it was hospitable.

*   *   *

Next day he took note of the animals. Paints, Sorrels, and quarter horses, a solitary Mustang; there were those even-tempered and those belligerent. Some were muscular, wiry, others stocky. Some whinnied at the slightest provocation, others silent no matter what. Weird but it was a pleasure for David to be around living creatures who could not speak.

He got right to work. Donned dirty overalls and trudged into the yard, shoveled droppings into a wheelbarrow and lugged it to a wide field, task took 'im several trips. He pitched hay onto the floor of the stalls for the hungry animals. After that he fetched water from a well 'round back, filling the troughs. Brushed down one of the sorrels that had gotten itself nicked-up on a long ride. Some men would shy from such work. McClure liked it fine. He was of a mind to embrace the drudgery.

That evening it cooled down considerable and he got his bunk made up. When the geezer was gone into his own cabin, the blond smoked and tended to his weapons, which needed as much care as any horse. Then he bedded down, sleeping with animals under the broad sky of a dark night.

*   *   *

He dreamed about the war the first night at the corral. He spent the better part of sixty-four in Northern Tennessee, fighting to retake Nashville. It had been the first notable Southern town captured by the Yankees, back when. Confederate leaders sent John Bell Hood to challenge the unionists and he seemed to be a most capable General. The blond had seen him up close, he was a fair-enough-looking man, with dark eyes and a long beard that made him look like a character in the Bible dressed in gray. He had lost an arm at Gettysburg and part of a leg at Chickamauga and still had fight left. This made the boys love him. His strength as a commander was moving folks around, deployment they called it. He had the laudable hope of out-flanking the blues, entering the city, and liberating it.

General Hood's great blunder was ordering frontal assaults, a damnable thing. He made the first mistake of placing a Brigadier name of Curry on his left. Yankees had no trouble whatsoever turning his position and making Rebel soldiers run. Hood responded by ordering charges at fixed positions, which was a terrible bad idea. The Battle of Nashville was a disaster and the southern army, half its men dead and goodly numbers wounded, was no more.

McClure and his Missoura bunch had the dire task of fighting in the center of the Gray army. Thus they took hell from Union artillery brought into gaps in Confederate lines. When the artillery stopped, Rebs faced volley upon volley of Minies. They called it the Battle of Nashville. It was not a battle, was not even a fair fight, it was being on the wrong end of a turkey shoot.

In the dream, McClure and his bunch reached breastworks of lashed, sharpened logs. Fancy officers called 'em *cheval de fries*, French term, though no common soldier knew that. David was with Mike Miles from Terrette County and a hardened fighter. The two were shooting and gabbing.

"The south's soon to be a memory," is what Mike said.

"Not if we drive them out of Nashville." McClure was not much of a patriot for the cause in waking life, but now in the dream he was. He raised his breech loading Yellow Boy, and shot a creeping blue foolish enough to stand tall.

"Quick Stop!" Mike Miles yelled and shot a Yank himself. Seemed the two could kill blues all day, turn the tide of battle. Just then an artillery shot hit nearby, *whomp*. The explosion sent out hot, sharp metal that hit Mike top to bottom, and bloodied him dead. He lay on the dark earth in a queer position, tangled.

Mike was dead but that did not stop him from talking. "We ain't been the same since Stonewall died," he said softly, referring to Stonewall Jackson, famous man, killed by mistake by his own men at Chancellorsville in '63. "God bless the South," he added then was silent like the dead should be.

*   *   *

David never had no religion. His childhood was hard-scrabbled, with father gone then mother gone, then him on his own. Schooling was minimal, he knew there was an alphabet and things called vowels, he could not read except for a few words here and there. He had seldom been inside a church, so when it came to religion all he knew was what folks showed, the way they acted having it. From that, he figured religion a thing he could do without.

One fact certain, fateful events were now unfolding. He was not in control of anything, rather was reacting to everything. All he could do was believe, if only in the moments of a day. Struck him that was what religion was, though he allowed he was likely mistaken.

*   *   *

After days of the most laying-low a man could do, corral boss told him to take a spell off, that it would do him good. "Go on down to Topeka, you will not believe the bustling thing the old cow town has become," Earl intoned. McClure was obliged to obey. While the notion sounded risky to the outlaw, it would be even more suspicious not to go. After all, a country boy from Kentuck could not resist city sights.

So David ventured on a cool, cloudy Sunday. His looks had changed during his time in Indian country. His hair fell to his shoulders and he was bearded. That and being dressed in deerskin made him look like a trapper of furs, or an Indian scout - anyone but the slick outlaw McClure.

Thus he was at ease ambling down a muddy side street 'til it reached Main. That's where Topeka proper began: Saloons, general stores, apothecaries, banks, hotels, brothels, this town had them all. He reached a landscaped square of public land. There stood a stone, columned edifice that was the state capital. This choice locale was also where rich folks built their abodes in rows along the road. The homes of the rich looked like the mansions he'd seen in Georgia and Tennessee, except here in Topeka they were set close, one after the other like fancy dominos. Sure the rich knew how to live, if proximity to other rich be the measure.

McClure moved off to a pony railing where he could lean back, have a smoke, gander, and be left alone. The weather cleared and the sun broke in the sky. Even on the Lord's Day, Main was a jumble of folk getting in each other's way, going about this and that. Conveyances abounded: buggies rolled by, so did the noon stagecoach, and then came an undertaker's carriage with a pine box on its flatbed.

David was paid the least mind by no one, like he was not visible. To townsfolk he was not a man with a price on his head, rather a stable boy on free time. He smoked and thought about his life. Seemed clear to him that his fate was to die hard, wheels were well in motion toward that end. Yet he was alive this day, here he was, a commoner, he could almost forget the killing. He was changed for sure, the running he'd done had humbled him.

Finished smoking, he ambled on. Came upon a saloon in an alley, brightly though poorly painted sign called the place *Whitehorse*. He stepped on in. Not much at all, cedar log walls and a long bar, floor full of sawdust. There were pine tables and chairs. Ceiling was low, nary a window, the place was dark away from the door, so lamps were lit throughout. Piano player was at work, tinny music emanated. Tables and chairs were occupied by a clientele of drunkards and others, some rowdy, some quiet. The blond sat furthest away from goings-on. Took off his hat, tussled his hair and proceeded to sip ale. *Whitehorse* also served stale bread and butter, free of charge long as you kept drinking.

Presently, he noticed a girl. Hadn't seen her come in before. She emerged from shadows and stood at bar's end looking back at the blond. Just like that she sashayed to his table and motioned at an empty chair.

"This seat taken?" she asked.

Being suspicious by nature, he barely acknowledged her presence. "Looks empty," he replied distractedly.

"May I join you?"

He did not rightly know what she meant. Only join he knew was to join the army. What did this dumb girl intend to say? "You want to sit?" he asked.

"I do indeed."

"Darling, I'm not a man to pay for the company of a woman," he said though it wasn't true, he'd paid plenty of times for a woman. The girl got a look and stepped back like she was mightily offended.

"I am not a working girl."

"Ain't you?"

"I am not. My father owns this place, you're a stranger, and I'm friendly."

She was also shapely, as blond as he, and a looker. No reason for him not to talk to her. "I apologize for the misunderstanding," he said, though he was not a man to say the words convincingly.

"Apology accepted."

"Have a seat, if you please," he added.

"Thank you kindly," she replied and did.

Piano player across the room was tickling keys to a tune about a boat sailing the ocean's blue seas. The girl tapped the tabletop with her fingers, acting happy. "I love this number," she said.

"I shouldn't have said you were a whore," he offered.

"You did not say it, you implied it," she stated.

He had no idea what that meant. All he knew she wasn't offended that he assumed she was a whore. She kept on tapping the tune, singing a line about the cutter as it sailed through rolling seas to safe harbor. David cast his eyes sideways at 'er. She wore snug clothes, showing off her fine body. Perfume made it over to him, commanding attention. "What's a gal like you do?" he asked with interest.

"Do?"

"In this here town."

She tilted her head, curious-like. "Lots of things. I knit and crochet. I read and write letters. Sometimes I help my father, like today. Got two younger brothers to take care of, no Mom, so as you can see I'm busy."

"I would say you are."

"What do *you* do?"

"Tend horses."

"I'll say you're good at it."

"How would you know?"

"I sense that you have a gentle but firm way with animals." It was she who had the way - here was a lass who understood plenty. Her lively smile made him recall his girl, the unfortunate one who got herself shot. Never did get her name, just like he never knew his Pawnee squaw's name. Couldn't let that happen again.

"What do they call you?" he asked.

She shifted in her chair while keeping time with the music. She was pleased with the question, took her time answering.

"They call me Nicky, how about you?"

He didn't answer straight off. Likely she was thinking he was the funny sort who was playing, leading a girl on. In fact he needed a moment to remember what his name was. "Name's Haddix," he said, "out of Oakridge, Kentucky."

She nodded like of course that was his name. She offered her hand and he took it. They shook hard. "Pleased to meet you, Mr. Haddix," she stated.

He almost smiled. They sat together for a spell, taking in the lively scene. Cowhands were drunk enough to knock over their own chairs. There was a really fat whore in a blue wig throwing handfuls of peanuts at tables of drovers. The ale was notably potent, and the whiskey was cheap.

Nicky waved across the room to an older fellow behind the bar. David figured it was her father. Man seemed none too interested in who his daughter kept company with. Even how he was both serving cowboys and groping a barmaid. Reminded David of his own father, damn him to hell.

"Mr. Haddix," she intoned out of the blue, "care to walk a girl home?" For sure this gal had a way. Holds her head down shy-like, even as her flashing eyes quicken the pace of men.

"If you've a mind to leave, I'll walk with you," he offered.

So the two left the saloon. Weather had cooled down considerable, wind coming in from the plains. She kept talking 'bout this and that as they made their way. The girl could chatter. She spoke of knitting, said that according to the ancient Greeks, it was the purest art form, and then she spoke of the proper way to catch trout and gut it. Then she went on about Reconstruction, the blond had nary a clue, something to do with the country after the war, and changes that were happening. Entire towns and counties had to be rebuilt out of smoky ruins. For sure easterners were coming in, Feds wanted black folks to vote, other baffling notions. David cared a whit about Reconstruction. Still, he did not mind Nicky's yapping. Some enticing gal she was who expressed herself so freely.

They did not head off to her place which was near the courthouse. Instead, she got the idea to see where he did his tending of horses so they went to the corral. A good walk away, she spouted on various subjects as they traversed. Upon arrival, she took in the place and then said she wanted to climb the rickety stairs up to his loft. Said it would be an adventure. Once in the loft, she tread into shadows, wound up pressed against the wall planks. By then she stopped talking, blinked up at him who had followed her. He put a hand around her small waist. Barkeep's daughter had desire and he was obliging.

*   *   *

The Marshal's office was a short distance from Topeka's main square. Quinn was there, feeling like foul weather. He had been removed from the comforts of his homestead for weeks. On the road, sleeping in woods, it was a sorrowful situation so far from civilization, left him with aching bones. What he and his posse were doing were their jobs. He had hoped to track down Jesse or Frank James or Cole Younger, who the marshal knew personally. Hell, he would take any member of the villainous James gang. He had entertained the pleasantry of riding his mount onto Main, holding in one free hand the reins of a trailing horse with a wanted outlaw laid over the saddle dead as a mole. He fancied the *desperado* dripping blood into the dust, even as a gathering crowd gawked and applauded his heroics. It was not reward money that fired Quinn up, he had money. It was not the idea of serving the citizens of the state. It was the hunt - he was a natural-born hunter. Didn't matter if it was man or beast. Some men find excitement in war, he found thrilling tracking down living things.

This hunt he came up empty. Contrary to hope, the marshal was having no luck with outlaws. Jesse Woodson James and his boys hit a bank in Cuthbert County three weeks before and it was thought they headed north afterwards, they left a trail. The marshal figured they'd run to western Nebraska and Sioux country. Him and his boys went there, though they did not cotton traveling too deeply into Redman land. The heavily armed posse found no sight of the gang, the faint trail they initially followed went cold. There was the marshal, left to himself in the backcountry. The James Gang had plain disappeared. The posse got lost to boot coming back, forced to backtrack after heading up a wrong valley head. They ran out of the dried venison and salted cabbage they'd brought, adding to the burdensomeness of the endeavor.

Lawmen were not aided in the least by common folks in the territories. Truth was the opposite, Jesse was a hero and the Law was corrupt. Countryside folks liked the gang and respected them. The outlaws robbed banks and railroads, taking rich men's money. In addition, the James boys were veterans of the rebellion, even if guerrillas, and the Border States had plenty of bitter secessionists, hard losers all. On the other hand there were those law abiding and God fearing folk who condemned the outlaw life. For them it was fear of reprisal that kept their mouths shut.

Quinn and the boys returned home empty-handed, having spent the better part of a moon's cycle on a fruitless chase. The territories are harsh. It rained and sleeted, the wind blew weighty branches off tall trees that the posse dodged. There was lightning and thunder some evenings so that none could sleep proper. Next day the sun would be hot as hell and the air would be alive with pesky bugs that flew into men's noses and ears.

For sustenance after they ran out of proper vittles, it was mostly rabbit, Lord how much rabbit can a man eat? The Marshal got constipated, which made him surly. To make himself shit he drank boiled birch root. Wound up shitting the better part of two days, which furthered his surliness.

Thus since Connor Quinn's return to civilization, deputies gave him a wide berth. It was taking a while for him to reclaim his comforts. Deputies nodded in agreement with anything he said, it was "Morning, Marshal," or "Evening, Marshal," with no one holding his terrible gaze. All except Jackson, who had been with him the longest, nigh twenty years, and was familiar with his ways.

*   *   *

Now the two were stationed directly across from spanking City Hall. Along the frontage, a group of men were at labor. Quinn and Jackson watched workers hammer at scaffolding. It was to be a hanging place. Staccato bangs of hammer strikes echoed through the square. Jackson let go a spit of tobacco juice then wiped his mouth with a shirtsleeve. Quinn was puffing on a corncob pipe. He took it out of his mouth and used the stem to point at the workers across the way.

"Those fellows are from Nebraska, I can tell, they are good at getting in each other's way. They don't have one brain between them."

Jackson spit, wiped his moustache. "Yep."

"Got a length of Georgia hemp for the hanging, I'll bet five dollars the cross-beam of that platform gives before the rope."

Jackson laughed though Quinn did not say things in a humorous way. The deputy tugged at his twin six-shooters. The Marshal blew a cloud a smoke into the air and cleared his throat.

"Jackson," he said and looked up into the sky.

"Yes sir."

"I'm tired of hanging cattle rustlers and horse thieves, and I'm tired of chasing Missoura bastards."

The deputy said nothing, then stated "We could go after McClure."

Marshal got a look on his face. "Who is that?" he asked and batted his eyes.

"Hired-gun been running wild."

"The one who kilt dead the beloved Sheriff Bailey?"

"Him."

"I recall now, the no-account you let get away in St. Joe."

The deputy got wide eyed, choked some on his chew then steadied himself. "Didn't happen like that, he ran before I could challenge him."

The marshal snorted "Oh that's right," like he didn't believe a word of it.

"Anyways, you said Bailey was an over-blowed hero."

Quinn laughed and did not reply. No love lost or found for the lawman Bailey, rest in peace. Jackson was too slow to know a joke when he heard one.

Marshal waved at the air. "McClure you say. That boy is long gone, no way would he be caught in either border state. I reckon he's in Canada by now." The deputy nodded at the fierce lawman and Connor Quinn turned his attention back to the construction of the hanging place.

At that very same time the wanted man they spoke of was across the street, thirty feet from the law. It was what eggheads call ironic. The blond sat under an elm, crossed legged like an Indian, watching workers hammer.

*   *   *

The Grand Event, the hanging, took place that Saturday. It was a warm, bright, October day. The man to be hung was a horse thief name of Nowitski or some such strange name. He was not a native-born American; neither did he speak English much. It was said his language was Hungarian, or maybe Romanian. It *was* known that he was the kind who could not help but steal horses and try to sell them. He had served prison time in Hays, a rough place. That did not cure him. Recently convicted in Topeka, he was about to be punished in a way that would assure he would not steal again.

Seemed like the entire town came out that day. Perhaps it was the fine weather; maybe it was the presence of an eight-piece band from Portland County, which regaled one and all with popular tunes. Most likely it was because Kansans enjoyed a hanging. The scaffolding was across the street from the courthouse where shiny new red, white, and blue buntings fluttered. God bless the Union.

The crowd attending was arranged just so. Furthest away from goings-on were polite folk, men in suits and their women in dresses. The men smoked and gabbed and held hands up over their eyes to see into the distance. The women twirled parasols against the sun and waved fancy-colored fans into their made-up faces. Being a distance away from the coming gruesomeness, these folks could remain above low entertainment while still witnessing the spectacle. The wide street at the scaffolding was filled with commoners and churchgoers. To them hanging was the triumph of American justice, straight out of the Bible, the word of God.

Closest to the hangman's rope was a disparate group. There were wide-eyed youngsters who, lacking supervision and even common sense, found a hanging great fun. Also close were strange folk, mostly men who'd never seen a neck stretched. Those boys were deemed sick in the head and were seldom invited to community socials. Lastly were officials of Topeka, that is, The Law. That day there was the mayor, sundry city elders, various upstanding businessmen, and Marshal Quinn.

McClure was present, up front. There was a force inside making him more than passing curious. As he believed a hanging was in his future, he desired to witness one. He was leaning against a post of the scaffolding. A deputy told him to move away just in case the construction toppled. Seemed an unlikely happenstance, but the blond wanted no confrontation, so he complied.

A set of steps led to the raised platform, where four men stood. One was Nowitski, who had a distant look about him, like he really wasn't there. He was a brown haired, sloped shouldered man, who was barefooted. Present too was a mumbling preacher toting a bible. Standing next to him was a fat man reading the charges against the accused and the decision of the court. As he couldn't read so well, it was taking a good while. Folks were laughing as he mispronounced words like "jurisdiction" and the phrase "incumbent upon authority," until finally somebody threw a stick of horse droppings at the poor fellow.

Hangman stood away from the rest. He was a short gent who wore the traditional black hood so that no one knew who he was though everybody knew it was Mr. Munson. He was a teacher at the primary school when he wasn't pulling levers and dropping men into the next life.

The fat man concluded: "So it is the order of the court of the great state of Kansas, that the accused, Manfred Nowitski, be hung by his neck until such time as he is pronounced dead."

The band finished up a song "When I Wake in Heaven," then the musicians stopped playing. They didn't leave though, they were curious like everybody. The crowd, which had been raucous, got solemn quiet, knowing what was coming. The preacher mouthed words from his holy book, nary a glance at the gathering. Hangman got close and spoke into Nowitski's ear, offering him what he held in his hand, that is, a burlap hood. Most condemned choose to wear the hood, sparing the spectacle of their twisted faces. Nowitski waved a hand, said something loud in a language no one understood. He refused the damn burlap. At that point the court-order-reader shrugged. "Have it your way," he uttered and left. Following suit, the preacher patted the condemned man on the back and departed.

Manfred was alone with Munson. It was as quiet in the square as in an empty church. All the folks - the polite in back, the gang up front - fixed their eyes on the platform. The schoolteacher placed a length of rope just so around the man's neck, adjusting the knot. Nowitski stood up straight and proud-like, hands fixed behind his back. He stared straight ahead. Here was one defiant man. Munson stepped over to a wooden lever, then he looked down to where the Mayor and Marshal stood gawking. It was the Mayor who gave the go-ahead.

The lever was pulled. The trap door that the bare-footed Nowitski was set on gave way. He dropped like a sack of potatoes. Falling a short distance fast, he then stopped just as quick with a snap along the length of his body. The rope tightened even more, then twanged as he jerked.

Crowd made a noise, combination of gasping, applause, and calls to the Lord in heaven. Manfred swung in a sad arch, face red and swollen. He bobbed like a cork on a fishing pond. His eyes stayed open and got large. Face made a sight unfit for Christian folk, which was likely his intention in refusing the hood.

McClure got a good look. Proper folks, including the mayor, shuffled from the town square with the show over and all. David kept on staring at the swinging man. He reached up with a hand and rubbed his own neck, though he wasn't aware he did. The dead fellow creaked for the dwindling crowd that afternoon.

IV

Once he believed he knew where McClure was holed-up, Thom was obliged to pursue. He could not pass the task to another. Strange the fugitive running where the Marshall resided, made Thom think that just maybe there was something personal between them.

He left Lawrence one morning with the rising sun, riding thirty miles on horseback to his destination. It was an easy journey, the weather was kind. The sheriff took a well-traversed route 'til he neared town, then he left the road for verdant foothills of passable terrain. Thus when his mount descended to flat land it was on the less-developed side, the outskirts.

He removed his badge, pulled his collar up and ambled streets, thus reconnoitering. Came upon the very center of Topeka, where city hall stood in an expanse of woodland, ponds, and footpaths. The green land was bordered on three sides by fancy homes, most impressive structures. Main Street with its full array of shops and goings-on ran from the square. Thom had not been in Topeka since before the war, it was surely now bustling. Good place for a wily one to lose himself.

Up one side of Main and down the other he strode. Entered saloons he did, to have a look-see at the clientele. Even visited a bordello, for which Thomas had no partiality. He made up an excuse to the Madam for being there, asked about a friend of his, David, tall blond. It was passable acting but to no avail. He stopped by an undertaker, told the man he had a dead relative coming in by train for burial. Undertaker got excited, he seemed to love his job. Powell asked folks harmless questions, here and there, small talk, all to the end of finding his man.

Second day of searching, he followed a hunch. He left the town's center and rode his mount to the periphery. He did not pretend to know McClure, the man was a puzzle, but he knew his fondness for horses. He'd been a pony rider, sure, but it was more than that. Thomas thought on the horse McClure inexplicably shot, though he seemed right partial to the beast. This outlaw was not like others, likely to do the unexpected. Good thing the sheriff had encountered his share of savvy men.

It was midday and he came across a corral on the south edge of town. An old man ran the place, said his name was Earl. Thom told him that his horse needed tending while he traveled by rail and asked if he could have a look around at the accommodations. Old man said sure and waved him to the stalls. Powell made his way up to the loft. There he came across bedding and clothing and then found the repeater rifle that was taken from his office during the jail break.

All that was left was waiting for McClure's return.

* * *

In the loft, biding time, Thom held an object in his hands. He rolled it over on his palm, acknowledging the craftsmanship. The object was a polished green stone, Baili said it was crafted jade. It was a man in robes, sitting cross-legged with hands in his lap. Smooth and whorled, cool to the touch, the statue had drooping ears and hair such that it might have been a helmet. The thing sat in heavenly repose, a mystery. Baili gave it to him when he left, said it was *Buddha*, that it belonged to her beloved father. She said it would protect him. He did not know who Buddha was, though she did explain some. He accepted the thing in the spirit in which it was given. He treasured it, keeping it in his vest pocket over his heart.

* * *

Sheriff was sitting on a rickety crate next to a window looking down at the only road, commanding the field of vision. He was well armed and stocked. It was a cloudy damp day in Topeka, the air smelled of wet earth. He'd been waiting a while, no idea where his quarry might be.

It was then, just like that. At the far end of the approach road, near the river's bend, a man made his way on foot. It was McClure. Last time he saw the outlaw, he was clean shaven and dressed in *chaparajos* over Reb pants. This version of the man, bearded and wearing deer skin, made a peculiar sight.

Thom pinned his badge back on and eased his way down the unsteady steps leading from the loft. Now in the corral he moved off into the stalls' shadows, not afeared of the horses giving him away. He too had a way with mounts and had introduced himself upon his arrival. Now the lawman hid in an empty stall. By-and-by McClure entered the dusty space, head down, striding to the loft. Thomas could see he was unarmed save for his tucked blade, there was no reason to wait. "David McClure," he said simply as he emerged into the light with his Spiller & Burr. The blond did not move a muscle nor turn around.

"Name is Haddix," he said.

"Don't think so."

"From Kentuck way."

"You are not Haddix to a man who knows you."

The wanted-man was cool and canny. He pivoted slow, barely raising an eyebrow. Now facing the lawman, he did not seem surprised by events, though he must have been.

"Hard Ride," he said.

"Last time I saw, you were in a cell."

"Don't take to those."

"Take that knife and toss it a good distance." Without another word, the man lifted the blade from the knotted leather of his belt and tossed it yards away. McClure stepped to the Sheriff, who reacted by pointing his pistol direct. The blond held a hand up like he wanted to talk some.

"Do not shoot me."

"You just keep your hands out where I can see them." McClure complied. "What's on your mind?" Powell asked.

"Why in creation you keep coming? I know it ain't reward money." Thomas both stood tall and was wordless. "So why do you do it?" David inquired.

The conversation seemed pointless. Wasn't the answer obvious? "I'm Sheriff of Lawrence."

137

Blond was one to scoff at high-mindedness. "Nonsense is what that is."

"Why you boys keep coming at Shiloh?"

David got a look at the mention of that place. He considered the question. "No sense starting a fight without finishing it," he offered.

"You are a tough man, and you are my prisoner."

"Appears so."

"Afraid I have to bring you to Marshal Quinn."

"Why be afraid of that?"

"I know the man," the sheriff said.

McClure nodded like he understood, though he did not. He seemed calm, and Thom was thinking damn if he didn't seem too calm, when just then he felt the cold steel of a gun's barrel smack against the back of his neck. Someone was directly behind him. David got happy. "Guess it's not my day to get caught," he said and gave a Rebel yell that echoed against the ceiling beams, quite a show of emotions from a stoic man.

Powell felt the steel behind him push hard. If he did not drop his pistol, he would be shot at. "You know what you gotta do, Sheriff," the blond offered.

Situation slowed time, he had moments to think. Could he make a move on the gunman, then turn back to the outlaw before he had a Bowie stuck in him? He determined he could not. He extended his arm and dropped the Spiller into the corral's dust.

Quick as you please, McClure bounded up the steps. The gunman kept the barrel pressed on Thom. The blond came back down in a hurry, though stocked and armed. Then he picked up his knife, tucked it back. "Make no mistake I should kill you, can't though," he said.

The lawman had no need to speak. He was wondering about the gun in his neck, curious as to who held the weapon. McClure saddled the nearest rested mount. It was a solitary Mustang, a strong animal.

Real serious-like, the blond gathered his saddlebag and checked his guns. When he was fully prepared, McClure looked to the person holding a gun on his would-be captor. "I want to thank you," he called out in a kind voice. "You keep this man here. He's a fine rider but so am I, with a head start I'm gone."

He grinned like a captured man now free. Hopped on his mount he did, gave a swift kick, the animal clumping out and running onto the narrow road north. McClure was gone.

Moments passed then the sheriff spoke. "I'm gonna step away and turn around slow," he began with hands raised. "Do not fire."

He faced the gun. While Thom was not a man to be easily surprised, in this case he was. There was a fine-looking blond girl in a green dress, holding a Paterson derringer. The weapon was a one shot special, more suitable for parlor tricks than killing.

"Who are you?" the lawman asked.

"I'm no one," she said with her tiny gun pointed, "I'm the one holding this weapon on you."

Thom would not disrespect a serious situation; but he could not help but smile. The girl was one hundred pounds soaking wet and her weapon was the size of a half-used bar of soap. Still, no fool was the lawman. He stared at the girl and she returned the gaze, then he looked up into the loft as if he spotted something. Her eyes followed in reflex. At that moment he swept his left hand, grabbing her wrist. The derringer went off with a pop and a wisp of white smoke. The piece of lead hit with a thud the thick center beam of the corral's ceiling. Her one-shot weapon was now as useless as it looked fully loaded, though this time it really was useless. Thomas twisted the wrist until she dropped the gun. He kicked it away as she rubbed her hand.

"That hurt," she scolded as if it was he who'd done something wrong.

"I imagine it did."

"You should apologize is what you should do." As tears welled in her eyes, Thom judged that she was McClure's local girl and not at all formidable. The sheriff picked up his pistol. "I'm a lawman," he said, "What you did was against the law."

"Lawman, how could I know?"

"See this badge?"

"How could I from the back? I thought you wanted to rob Mr. Haddix."

"From Kentuck," he said ruefully.

"Handsome fellow that just rode out of here, are you stupid?"

"I am not, that buck's name is McClure."

"No Sir."

"You should get your facts straight before you spout them."

"Listen here, my father is an important man."

"What's he do?"

"Owns a saloon."

"Don't sound so important."

"He dines with Marshal Quinn, they deer hunt together. When he learns that you nearly broke my entire arm . . ."

"Miss, I have no time for blather, I will say two things. First of all, never try to kill when you do not know how. It is bound to turn out bad."

Thomas walked over to the derringer, picked it up and threw it up into the loft, just in case this wiry gal had another bullet somewhere. After he holstered his Spiller, he turned back to her.

"What's the second thing you got to say?" she asked with her nose in the air and her arms akimbo, like she was better than him. That made Thom mad enough.

"Second thing is not words," he offered.

"Then what is it?" the blue-eyed firebrand remained defiant. Thom hit her with a fist to the jaw, a short punch, just so. She was knocked back, a real queer look on her face. Her eyes rolled, then closed. She was out on her feet. The sheriff caught the girl before she could fall; he lowered her to the dirt.

Took minutes for him to saddle his own mount and be off after Haddix.

V

Ignorant opine there's little to riding 'cept doing it. Mount assuredly, give a kick, keep balanced. That notion is wrong-headed. Man riding badly makes a poor sight, worse, he brings peril. Bouncing foolishly on the muscular creature's hindquarters could well cause injury to man and beast. Besides all that, one gets nowhere fast.

Powell was on a hard ride. He was used to those, like it was an acquaintance. Pony riders rode eighty miles a run, difficult to imagine such a feat nowadays. Consider the strain on a boy's body, and on the animal being ridden. If the rider did not pace the effort and account for the horse's temperament, he was sorely pressed.

This day he pursued McClure on the road north along the Kansas River toward Concordia. The sky was gray and the road lay out ahead of him in slowly winding turns. The outlaw was miles ahead but left a trail, no secret where he'd run. Thom knew the blond would be pushing his animal to the limit.

He kept low on his horse, patted its neck as it ran down the road fast enough to kick up clumps of dried mud. After riding in a gallop, he pulled back into a three beat-gait, that is, a canter. Horse could manage such a pace. Along the road the two moved in a rhythm like the beating of native drums.

*   *   *

Passing the time, he pondered one terrible fight serving the Union. It was June of sixty-five, he and handpicked troops rode hard from Dyersburg, Tennessee. They moved clear through the state of Missouri, to Lawrence, Kansas. It was a hot three-day journey, in windy, merciless weather. They rode with good reason.

Union spies had determined that none-other-than William Clarke Quantrill would be passing along the county road, heading to Wichita. His intention was to flee the justice of the Union, hide in the backcountry. It was the intention of the blues to combine forces with local Kansan partisans and turn the tables on the infamous bushwhacker. The plain plan was to attack him and his men at the place where years earlier they had done their massacre of Kansans. Thus would be the justice that would end his damned shameful life.

Powell was a sergeant at the time. In command was Colonel Winston, a tall and well-proportioned officer who attended West Point. He was an able commander in appearance only. Though undoubtedly a brave fighter, he was the reckless type and worse he drank to excess, which affected his judgment. Affected his balance too as the man was known to fall off his own horse.

During the ride to meet Quantrill, none of the boys talked much. It figured to be a bloody fight. If this famed criminal was cornered, he'd die fighting, he was not the surrendering kind. With Sergeant Powell was a corporal name of Ben DeCamp, a most able man. The Union boys arrived at the crossing of Whicker County Road and the road to Wichita well ahead of the Rebels. They established a perimeter for the ambush and hid themselves real good. The place was thickly wooded, suitable terrain.

Thom and Ben had fought side-by-side at Chickamauga, a murderous fight. Now the two tended their weapons at camp, doing what soldiers do: wait in quiet dread for shooting to start.

"Don't suppose those Jayhawkers know how to fight," Ben stated. He was referring to the locals aiding the Union.

"No, suppose not," Thomas replied.

The corporal was looking for more assurance. "They must fight some."

"They know how to shoot and are in goodly numbers, should be enough."

"Least they're down the road, can't shoot us."

They had a dark laugh.

*   *   *

The ambush was U-shaped. Quantrill's bunch would be free to ride on up County Road. There was a homestead, Wakefield's

Farm, which provided headquarters for the blues. The guerrillas would be attacked from there.

At the open end of the trap were the locals, Kansans itching for a shot at those who murdered their townsfolk two years in the past. The partisans would be hidden in tall grass on either side of the way, tucked nicely behind post fences. When Quantrill rode into the U far enough, he would not be able to back out, the Kansans would have blocked egress. His last fight was fated to be short and bloody.

The moon was cloud covered, suitable for an ambush. Full moon allowed for overmuch visibility. If no one could see, the advantage went to the attackers.

Sure enough, 'round midnight, dead of night, they arrived. The approach of cantering horses was like low rumbling thunder. There they were, a group of fifty or so coming up county road. The raiders were a motley crew of men dressed in no uniform way, ragtag. Veterans all, mostly bearded, many long haired and hatless. At the lead was a group of four, set off from the rest, who seemed in capable charge. There was one in particular, thin and clean-shaved in a wide brimmed hat. When Powell spotted the man, just before hell broke loose, he had the notion that it was Quantrill himself. The unionists had no intention to give quarter so none was offered. Instead, soon as the head of the column of riders reached the homestead, they could plain see the road blocked by union supply wagons and men with guns. With that, shooting commenced. The fifty raiders received a smoky volley from a hundred rifles. The discharge roared into the night and echoed. Guerrillas fell off their horses by the handfuls and horses fell dead too. Above the sounds of shooting, pained cries of wounded men and animals could be heard.

Quantrill's boys were hardened fighters and ambush notwithstanding they fought back, sending hot lead of their own into the darkness around them. Some stayed on horseback shooting revolvers. Others dismounted, armed with repeater rifles. Colonel Winston, who should have known better, stepped out from behind a wagon to get better aim with his Colt. He got hit. A Minie turned him around like he was dancing. He dropped his gun and fell into the dust.

Kansan partisans were making a mess of things at their end, killing raiders but also winging each other as some fired carelessly across Whicker Road. One volunteer ventured too close and got hit by a roaring volley from the south side. He went flying into the wooden fence, crumpled up, calling out "Lordy, I'm hit." Several Jayhawks, just plain afraid, ran like rabbits into a cornfield away from the road. Still, other militiamen did their duty and kept shooting and advancing. Union soldiers tightened the noose on the front end, assuring that Quantrill's men would not be escaping with their lives.

The hard-pressed leaders, group of four, were off their mounts and fighting well, having already shot blues. Their coordinated fire carved a position for themselves on the edge of the road away from the wagons. After Thomas and Ben dragged the bloody-winged Winston behind a wide-spreading oak, they moved against the leaders. The sergeant and a squad of good men formed a line behind fencing. Their first volley took down two of the group; the second volley got a third member. Last man standing was the one with the wide-brimmed hat. That raider stood tall, cursing and yelling out to heaven. Thom cocked his pistol and stepped into the road for a clear shot. The man tossed down his rifle and drew his six-shooter. He strode at the sergeant, wanting to kill one more Yankee in his nefarious life. Thom fired a quarter-step before the man. The shot thudded into the Rebel, stopped him quick and knocked him back. He then got hit by fire from other blues. His pistol had gone off with a crack but to no avail. Hat flew into the air. The man, full of holes, fell into the roadside.

Fifty raiders deceased or stretched out in the dirt, shot up but alive. The Kansans commenced celebrating, firing in the air and whooping it up. Thinking there might be stray fighters snaking on their bellies trying to get away, Powell organized squads to search. Two army doctors rode with the blues, and they were set busy tending to wounded. Looked like Winston would make it, lucky.

* * *

Blues stood over the body of the last raider. He was a grim-faced corpse. "This here is William Quantrill himself," Ben said, adding "The Kansans want to hang him up in a tree."

The sergeant said nothing. He looked around at the dead men and horses. It was a small battle, but bloody enough. Made him sick some, as ambushes were not much honorable.

"I believe it was your shot did him in," Ben said sounding certain.

"Was hit nigh half dozen times," Thom testified. The corporal understood, there is no honor for a kill in the tangle of dead.

* * *

Fast out of the stables at the edge of town, David rode hard for a good hour, must have gone ten mile. The mustang was strong if moody, the blond did not pretend to know the beast, but it did like to run. He would have preferred to take the sturdy Quarter Horse, but it had been ridden earlier and was still sweated. This mustang was rested, it could be pushed. What he didn't know was how long Nicki could hold Powell. Hell, maybe she shot him, he allowed that unlikely and in truth hoped against it. Only sure thing: he was running again and tired of that.

Did not dare camp that night so he followed the hard riding with some at a slower pace. After that he dismounted and led his horse along the road where it forked toward Concordia. There he kicked up underbrush, tore branches from saplings in order to mislead anyone following. He found shallows and crossed the Kansas River.

Weather was cold with sharp blowing wind. He wished he'd taken time to bring gear suited for heading north. Woolen gloves, an extra blanket. He had not. McClure was no stranger to discomfort, so he regretted only in passing the haste with which he ran from the capital city.

He came out the shallows of the cold river no worse for wear. He dismounted and guided the mustang back onto the road. Now on the other side of Concordia he was happy to leave that cow-town behind. He had a strategy: if he skirted the settlement a following posse might guess he headed to town to lose himself among drinking and whoring miners. Though he figured the ruse would work on some, he knew Hard Ride would not be fooled at Concordia.

He tethered his horse, and walked a bit on his own, taking moments to ponder. He'd headed north out of the corral, it was the only road. Now he needed a plan. Thought came into his head to ride back to that Pawnee settlement, wasn't bad there, he was left alone and he had a squaw. He could picture her quiet, contented way, seated on rocks at creek's edge.

After resting and having a drink of water, David mounted his horse, gave a kick, and headed up the narrow road that led northeast to the Nebraska border. Mustang started snorting even as it galloped. It was like overmuch riding was unwelcome, cursed luck, it was a contrary animal.

As he rode his mind wandered to the Express. Pony riders knew that a willful horse was fine for a short run, perhaps even a preferred animal. He recalled a Paint he rode through Colorado Territory, that animal would not run proper, was like it did not want any part. As a result of horse-moodiness, the young blond was late into his station. That meant late leaving, late arriving in St. Joe. Stationmaster was mock-surprised: "Ain't like you, Davey," and he had a laugh at the boy's expense. Blond learned quick how to coax a contrary beast.

This day he was putting into practice lessons learned. He stopped his ride in the waning sunlight, hopping off fancy like he used to. He patted the mustang. He wasn't one to talk to a strange horse, so he didn't, but he took time to be kind. The two stood on the snaking road listening to nature's quiet. Cooling air and a good breeze assured it would be a cold night.

After a passable rest, the blond remounted and rode at an easy pace. The border was closing, miles away, hell McClure could have been in Nebraska already. He thought about the Pawnee squaw, promised himself that if he did see her again, he'd find out her name straight off and make her know his.

All he had to do was shake his shadow.

The outlaw camped 'round midnight, acknowledging necessity. Came to a spot off the road, tethered the Mustang and built a fire. Found a turtle at creek's edge. He cracked its hard shell on rocks, and then cut it up and cooked it in river water with nut grass. Turtle meat ain't bad at all. He was weary enough, but when he bedded down he could not sleep. He'd doze, then wake, hour after hour of fitfulness. Strange, he was under stars and the black sky yet it did not give peace like it ought to. His mind was not one, rather in pieces, so rest did not come. He waited for first light. When it arrived, he threw freezing river water on his face and neck, filled a canteen, saddled-up then rode on.

*   *   *

It was that afternoon, cold and windy, he was closing on Pawnee land. He felt danger nigh. He pulled up and gathered his senses. The mustang was snorting, breathing heavy. Did the animal sense trouble too? He stared at the horizon. Nothing but wild backland. The blond could hear his own heart beating. There was fierce wind whistling through trees and making sound trees do. They rustled like the ghosts of his fellows kilt in war. He stood in the saddle and gazed inland from the river, the horizon remained empty. What was causing the troubling feeling? Indian or Lawman or his own weakness?

Regardless, it served him to hasten, no sense worrying. If he was tracked down, shot dead, that was predestination, he knew that was coming his entire life. So he gave his mount a pat aside its long face, followed by a kick to get it going.

After a good spell of easy riding, he slowed his gait, gave a pull on the reins, stopping the ride. Still wary, he turned around in the saddle. That was when he spotted him at the skyline. He waited until he was sure, then he could see, mere mile or two away, a horseman silhouetted against the fading light. It was damn Sheriff Powell.

The blond shook his head, cursed, gave the mustang a swift kick with one spur, and galloped. Had taken the better part of two days for him to be found, found he was. It was the mount, had to be. Mustangs ain't worth much. Lawman had his own ride, a trusted animal that was as familiar as a favored weapon. McClure instead had the first ride available, damn his luck.

Then something clicked inside his head, he came upon a strong notion. He pulled the reins tight, bringing the horse to a stop in clouds of dust. He turned the mustang around and drew his revolver. It was best this way, he'd done terrible things, and it was better than hanging. Strict justice, there's a fit end. He decided to ride full tilt at his pursuer, make the sheriff shoot. That man was a fine marksman, he would get the job done.

*　　　*　　　*

Powell kept on the ride, alone in his thoughts. The road he travelled headed to Concordia where there was a fork away from civilization and toward Indian Territory. Tom figured the outlaw wanted nothing to do with Concordia, here was a no-account, piddling place where a stranger would be readily noticed and unwelcomed.

When the sheriff first captured McClure, he was wearing *chaparajos* over Rebel grays. Now it was deerskin, Indian garb. Thom was betting that McClure now rode to the Platte and Pawnee land. Did he have a girl there? Tarnation if the man didn't have a way with women.

Sheriff crossed the Kansas River. He pulled his collar up against the wind and tugged the brim of his hat down. Cold, rainy clime, unfit for a ride of any sort, much less a hard one in pursuit of a deadly fugitive. But his mount, a strong and fit Sorrel, was surely game.

He pondered ponies and one memorable ride during the Express. He was in Colorado Territory, coming back from California, when a freak snowstorm hit. The weather had been cold and clear, then the wind was blowing a chilling whiteness into his face. His mount was a fine horse, a bony, wide-eyed Palomino that could run all day. Mount and rider found themselves out in the open on the seemingly endless prairie. The wind and snow would not stop their fury. Presently hailstones the size of quarter dollars commenced hitting at sharp angles. He dismounted, there was no sense continuing because the road had disappeared into swirling white. He led the struggling horse on foot but in no direction he could determine.

In a matter of minutes the situation was desperate. Thom was not dressed for the hellish weather and no shelter could be found. His exposed skin was pelted with ice that hurt like stones. He pulled at the panicky horse with one hand, and grasped the mailbag with another. No mail had been lost by riders in the nine months of Express, he was determined not to be the first, but if man and beast didn't find shelter soon, lost mail would be the least of it.

Palomino stumbled in exhaustion, though it stayed upright. It snorted and spit. Wasn't more than a few steps when it dropped hard at a grouping of cedars, it was not going anywhere. The trees provided the slightest protection, so there was no sense in any course of action besides hunkering down next to the animal, draw heat from its body. He uttered a prayer, though he was not a young man to pray. Still, he did, keeping it simple: Lord, end this vengeful storm.

God was not to be found in the blinding swirl. The Palomino was quiet. He could tell it was dead. Weird, it should not have died, it was a strong, willing animal with true spirit. Thom felt for a pulse in the neck and found none. Nothing to do but carry on. He stood up and headed east, at least what he thought was east. He could no longer feel his extremities so good. He contemplated that it was destiny that he die young.

It was not. He kept trudging along the road. The wind abated, weather lifted, slowly at first then surely. The temperature moderated. With a clearing sky, the rider found the road to Cheyenne Wells. He waited hours there, near half a day. He drank melting snow and ate a bit of buffalo jerky. A stagecoach came along. He and his charge of mail were safe.

*   *   *

Sheriff did not mind daydreaming, kept his thoughts off the dangers ahead. Now he was on a ridge above the river. He had a feeling, one he trusted, that the man he was trailing was near. Powell had scant reason to believe he could catch up to McClure. His quarry had left a trail, though he was crafty and it was hard to follow what-with false leads. McClure knew how to run, nevertheless Thom believed the end was nigh. Rain stopped, there was cloud movement and clearing. Sun was setting, casting violet hues as curtains on the day.

He pulled his horse up, squinted into the distance, thinking he saw something. Then he rode harder until he was sure. There was a horseman on the plain down the slope from the ridge, had to be the outlaw. Strange, McClure was not moving on his mount, he had stopped. Sheriff eased his animal down the ridge onto the plain. The hillside was gravelly, the horse slide some. The animal was tired and sweating, as was its rider. Arriving on the plain Thom kicked his mount into a canter, patted the beast in assurance. He could see McClure clear as day.

The man was tall in his saddle, facing the oncoming sheriff. Some two hundred yards separated the men. Thomas pulled up his sorrel and stared, what the outlaw was up to was baffling. Then McClure doffed his hat in a greeting. It was not Powell's style but he repeated the acknowledgement.

After that the lawman saw the outlaw had his pistol drawn and held in the air. Thomas in a reflex did the same. McClure gave his horse a kick and came hard at Powell. What was this?

Was it a charge of horsemen, one last fight, Blue and Gray? Thom was perplexed, and angry, he did not want it to end thus. Didn't seem right, nor fated.

It was then unfolding action changed course. David spotted them first, along the ridge behind the lawman, he slowed his charge. Thom, seeing the outlaw looking, turned his head: there at the crest were Indians on black and brown mustangs and spotted ponies. Both men pulled up, bringing their mounts to a dust swirling halt.

The sheriff looked closer: *Lakota*. One did not need to know much about Indians to recognize a painted war party. The whites lived in border States, where they and Indians coexisted but did not mix. Powell and McClure were trespassing. The danger in the warriors' presence was apparent, each man had a new enemy.

Thomas put spurs to his horse's flank, closing the distance to the outlaw. The soldier in him reconnoitered. There was a grouping of shrub pines and smoke trees nearby. It provided an island of cover in the middle of the bare, flat plain. He headed there. Wordless communication and agreement took place, McClure got the idea. In moments the two were dismounted at the trees, even as the Indians made their way down the gravelly slope.

"Sheriff Powell," the blond acknowledged and dismounted. They tethered their horses to pines at the center of the outgrowth, the animals were jumpy, understandable. Repeater rifles were made ready. Both stood tall behind the minimal cover of trees, hardened fighters ready for the next hand to be played.

There were an even dozen in the Lakota party that rode up in clouds of dust. They were about as fiercely painted and heavily armed as they could be. All wore colored headbands, a few of them had feathered headdresses. Clad in buckskin pants with vests of beaded reeds, their bodies were painted with red and white, green and black streaks. They were full of vim as they reared their horses and then lined up their snorting mounts facing the stand of pines. Riders settled down, and things got still. Nuthin between them and the white men but a flat stretch of Nebraska plain.

"Indians follow you?" McClure asked.

The sheriff was offended and did not hide it. "I figure they spotted you and were laying low," he said.

"I ain't seen a brave, Topeka to here."

"You thought."

"Son, I don't get followed when I ain't aware."

"You are in the thick of Indian country."

"No such place, this is Union land."

The sheriff had no time for contrariness. Still, took his time speaking. "I see you're dressed like a native."

The blond looked at his deerskins and snorted. "Traded for these," he began. "I was with the Pawnee, cost me *chaparajos* and a good blade."

"Maybe the Pawnee betrayed you."

"Not them, didn't care a lick, they were decent like that."

"Perhaps the *Lakota* trailed you from the Platte, they are numerous thereabouts."

"I know when I'm being trailed. Felt *you* coming."

The sheriff did not see the use in arguing. "There they are, regardless," he concluded.

Blond half smiled. "You and me in the same fight, imagine that," the outlaw said. It was not a notion worth imagining. McClure was a desperate man, facing a hanging soon as he was caught. Powell had plenty to live for.

Lakota did not waste time. The band separated into two groups of six braves. They gave their ponies a kick and took off. Strong and hard they rode, one after the other in a galloping line. They proceeded to create a circle that surrounded those holed up. As they galloped, hollering like Indians do, the circle tightened. They made no effort to use their weapons, did call out quite a bit though in words and yells. Seemed their intent was to scare daylights out of their quarry. With some men maybe, but not with two so well acquainted with dire circumstance.

Indians whooped over and again as they closed, tightening the circle. Not panicked a tad, the blond took his repeater, rested its barrel in the palm of his left hand. He stood straight and picked out an Indian riding, tracked him, waited and shot. Brave got hit, clean as a whistle, knocking him off the blanket that served as his saddle and onto the hard ground. The unfortunate man bounced in the dust to a face-down stop. His horse slowed and stopped and stood on the plain, surprised it no longer had a rider. Quite a shot, Thom could not help but admire.

"You shoot like that all the time?" He asked without wanting an answer.

"Can make that shot half the time," McClure replied.

The killing made an impression on the war party. Bucks hopped off their ponies and lifted their shot comrade, laid him across a horse's back. The rest of the party pulled up from their circle-riding. Leaders came together in *powwow*, gesturing among themselves. A tall brave with a fancy war bonnet yelled to heaven and shook a fist at the white men. For sure there was bad blood. Lakota must have figured there was no sense being target practice for a shooter like that. They rode in a common gait back to the base of the ridge.

The light of day was waning, the Indians set up camp.

*   *   *

Powell and McClure took stock, theirs was a situation both desperate and baffling. "What in creation them redskins want with us?" McClure inquired.

"They want to kill us," was all the lawman said.

Neither knew much about *Lakotas*. They were savage, but were not so common in Eastern Nebraska, where the Pawnee were settled. They were not found at all in Kansas and Missouri. Free roamers is what they were, did not like settlements so they did not like white people, who were the settling kind.

Thom was perplexed as to their motives. He did know that Lakota hated railroads, and would attack construction sites. Where track was laid, buffalo disappeared, as did the natives' way of life. There had been a famous treaty at Fort Laramie in eighteen fifty-one, which was supposed to ensure peace. Soon afterwards, settlers moved into Indian Territory, violating the treaty, and the federal government did nothing. Lakota chief named Red Cloud rightly claimed that whites broke the agreement. Since then "the good friends" had been on and off the warpath.

*   *   *

The men were well armed. Each had a rifle and a six-shooter, plus the sheriff had his five shot Paterson. McClure possessed his trusted Bowie. They had sufficient rounds of bullets for a good fight. Their horses were content enough at the center of the stand, though animals get nervous when men start fighting. The whites had water and modest portions of food.

Night was nigh. They could not have a fire, braves might well shoot arrows at the light. They hunkered down and bore witness to the Indians, who had a good blaze going. There was a one buck in a fine head-dress. He was in the center gesturing and having his say. Around him, braves were seated crossed-legged like natives do. One was smoking a long pipe, another had a short one. Even from the safety of the pine stand, puffs of smoke were seen in the air as pipes were passed.

*   *   *

As daylight failed and blackness settled in good, the *Lakota* made their move. First thing they did was put out their fire, sending plumes of smoke into the air, and casting the plain in long, darkening shadows.

Leaving their horses bound together at the base of the ridge, armed braves came forward on foot, their buckskinned forms barely discernable in faint light. What in tarnation were they up to?

War party stopped. One hundred yards or so separated red men from white. Light from the partial moon illuminated. By now it was plain enough to see: the Indians had not brought firearms. They carried only their bows and quivers of arrows. Hearts sank when the whites understood it was about to rain shafts with razor sharp tips. Waning light guaranteed poor vision and made prospects grim.

"Arrows won't get through these trees," McClure offered unconvincingly. The pines were some eight feet high. Crouched on the ground the men were protected. But branches were not thick or fully foliated. Arrows would sure get though. Then there was the danger to their horses. The animals were barely protected. Maybe the Indian plan was to kill the mounts, trapping the men. Not a bad plan.

Braves readied their bows. McClure commenced firing his repeater. Fact was he was shooting at shadows, crack shot or not. Meanwhile, arrows were let loose. First came a *ping* as pulled-back strings were released. Then a whirling hiss of increasing loudness. Arrows flew into the stand, through tree branches, sticking in the ground and trunks. Then others were loosed, striking pines and chipping bark. Surrounding trees were getting stuck left and right. Taking the lead from the outlaw, Thomas fired his rifle, this way then that. With gun smoke in the air, visibility was further cut. There were cracks of gunfire and hissing of arrows, the feathered

156

shafts rustled leaves of limbs. Frantic horses whinnied and kicked out their hind legs.

Indians were spreading, surrounding the stand. Braves fired from each angle they could and continued their blood chilling war cries as they closed in. The result was a most strangely fearsome attack.

Thomas judged it was the Indians' plan to kill their horses. He had started to crawl to the mounts with the intention of forcing them down into a safer position. Just then there was a horrible sound from the mustang. It reared up where it stood, let out the sharpest cry. It stomped the ground, kicked out its legs, stumbled then fell hard into the brush. The creature had been penetrated deep in the neck and chest with arrowheads.

The sheriff reached the mustang. It was dying, its eyes fixed open, tongue hanging. Blood flowed from the base of the shaft of one arrow stuck half the length into its neck. The horse was struggling for breath. Powell drew his Paterson, cocked, and put one bullet into the animal.

He stood up from a crouch and moved to his agitated, still-standing Sorrel. He spoke words of assurance, though words fell on deaf ears. He grabbed the reins and pulled, urging the animal to the earth. The horse, jittery afraid, knew what its rider wanted and reluctantly complied. Now on the ground, it was as safe as its master.

Rain of arrowheads continued. As the Indians closed in, their shadowy forms became better targets. McClure fired and the plaintive cry of a hit brave answered. Powell, with his back now to the outlaw, fired at a war cry with his repeater and silenced it in the middle of a whoop.

The braves backed away. The arrows slowed, then stopped. There were fading calls from the war party as they trod and danced proud-like to their campsite.

*   *   *

The two caught their breath, checking themselves for cuts or worse. It was dark now in the tree stand, just cloud-obscured moonlight. Through the night air, native voices could be heard at their camp. With their fire rekindled; they commenced parading around it. Sparks of light rose from the ceremony's flames, bringing flying bugs and bats to the glow's dark edge.

Likely the red men were celebrating their daring, a thing they do. It was folly to pick a fight with riflemen when all you brought was bow and arrow. Indians thought it most courageous. If a brave came back from such an attack unharmed, he earned the feather of an eagle. Touching an enemy, taking something from him, and living to tell the tale was a holy act for the tribe. They called it counting coup.

One thing sure, their arrow-charge was not only outlandish daring, it achieved an objective. They killed a horse and put the fear of God into men.

"Got holes in you, Sheriff?" David asked his companion.

"Couple scrapes," was all Thom said, then adding, "Your horse is dead."

"Did you end its misery?"

"I did."

"I'm saving a piece of lead, best not taken alive by redskins."

The lawman did not answer. His eyes adjusted to dark, he could see McClure had his shirt opened and there was an arrowhead piercing his side at the belt line. Partial tip came out his belly side. Flesh wound, but it looked none too good.

"First arrow I ever got, scared me," McClure stated. The laceration was fearsome, the outlaw was stoic. He took his blade, used the razor edge, and cut the shaft. He turned it slow, worked it out of the flesh. Then he removed the arrowhead, had to dig fingers in some. It must have hurt like hell on earth, but he was steely.

"Let's get some water on that," Thom advised.

"Prefer whiskey." They had a dark laugh. Powell cleaned the gash with water and then ripped his bandana to plug the bleeding hole. Not the best doctoring.

158

Meantime the Indians settled down. They wound up ringed around their campfire, there was mumbling *powwow*. Best the whites could do was quench thirst with water and keep an eye out.

McClure had a notion: "What's to stop us from getting out of here?"

"On foot?"

"Or with one horse. We make it to the river, the strong current will aid us. You know how to swim?"

"I do."

"I am a strong swimmer. What do you think?"

"You could make a run for it in your condition?"

"I've moved with worse than this."

"Those braves are alert. It's a good bit to the river, they get us in the open, and their ponies will run us down."

The blond thought at it. Nothing to be done. By and by, Indians' fire went out, even they needed sleep.

*   *   *

The sky cleared at dawn. A yellow sun began its creep into the east. Thomas stood tall, ever cautious. Attack would surely be soon. He did not cotton being hunted like some prize game, trapped in a confining space. Made him feel like a helpless and hapless critter, and he wasn't that. With dawn, his mind and heart were taut, ready for what was coming, be it unknown.

David, for his part, was the worse for wear. Bleeding had thickened and stopped around the gash. He was haggard like fighting men get. With effort he rose from the ground using a sturdy stick like a crutch. Thom took a step to help, but the blond's look stopped him.

Blackbirds swooped in the air, calling to each other as Powell and McClure watched the flat plain together. There was a brave out there. He was sitting cross-legged. On the earth next to him was the body of another brave that had been killed. At the foot of the ridge the rest of the war party was still camped.

"Man is guarding the dead," the blond uttered.

Thom nodded. "A kin, perhaps it's their religion."

"Git out."

"What?"

"Indians don't have religion."

"They do."

"Which?"

"Theirs."

David conceded the point. "Nonetheless, makes a weird sight."

Thom noted the warrior's devotion. The man lightly swayed, he was making a sound, took moments to understand he was chanting. Baili had described such praying. He pondered religion, what it meant to divers people. He touched his vest pocket and the jade Buddha.

*   *   *

The natives in camp stirred. The sun was brightening the sky as they broke camp and readied their mounts. Powell and McClure got steely for the coming fight. The blond had jerky and the two shared. That and sips of water was their sustenance. They had time so they sat on the ground, waiting and wordless.

Then Thomas spoke. "I have a question for you Quick Stop."

The blond waved at a bug. "What's that, Sheriff?"

"What made you take on killing?"

The outlaw got a funny look like he didn't understand the question though he did. He cast his eyes to the ground.

Powell kept at it. "The do-gooders, by any account they were harmless fellows."

David was surprised the lawman was so direct, though he conceded the man's smarts. He took his time, mumbled "ain't what I heard," then he decided might as well fess up some. "Killed for money, son," the blond said. "Damnable thing, I am aware. Back then, war over, no prospects at all. Seemed permissible to keep shooting and get paid. I know I will burn in hell."

"I would not take you for a killer," Thom stated.

"Hell of a thing to say, you know I've kilt."

"Killing in war is not murder, nor is killing a man in a fair fight. You had the advantage at the corral. Finish me and you buy yourself a lot of time to run. You left me to a girl with a toy gun. Odds turned in my favor."

Real quick, anger rose in McClure. He was looking pale, but it was like he was gaining strength. Stared at Powell. "You are looking at a bad seed, don't put goodness on me. I imagine that you have religion, I saw the statue you carry, strange thing, and the way you act with it."

The sharp words stung Thomas, and made blood come to his face. He was offended a man like McClure would make him think of his girl. Now *he* was angry. "You don't know a damn thing of which you speak."

Both men were familiar with hard words and squabbles, now was not the time. Thomas was willing to let a slight to the statue go. David was weak enough not to care one way or the other. They sat on the earth, real quiet, bugs buzzing, birds calling, the wind rustling pine boughs.

Just like that, David spoke up: "Met a no-account cowboy in a saloon, told me about a man in St. Joe, called him Boss, wanted fellows out of his way and was paying for the deeds," he started.

"Why did the big man want those folks dead?"

"I don't know, unless it was cuz of the Pony Express."

Those words surprised the Sheriff straight off. "What's that you say?"

"The do-gooders got in the way of money being made when the Yankee government had the rails carry mail."

True the Pony Express went bust in sixty-one even as railroads were booming. The Federals gave mail contracts to the rails and not to ponies. It was a big victory for the iron horse crowd and the death of the Express. Resulted in hard feelings and calls for fair justice. For divers folks, justice is vengeance.

Still, McClure's tale was a tall one to a plain-thinking man. "You may have been misled regarding the whys and wherefores," Thom said.

McClure let out a pained cough, he waved at the air. "Devil found me willing," he concluded.

Out in the flats the Lakota were ready.

*　　　*　　　*

The fervid war party was now on horseback. They cantered from their camp to their fellow watching over his dead comrade. That brave mounted, leaving the peaceful charge prostrate. Now the leader waved a command and they all got in single file and took off. No hurry, they separated and moseyed until they circled the whites. The horses and their riders were spaced just so. All the while some of them were making singsong noises, like they were weird-praying. Their anger shown too, bad blood. The display was frightful to witness. Thomas's faithful mount whinnied and stomped, something it normally did not do, like it knew what was coming.

"Looks like they mean to finish it," McClure stated.

The sheriff moved to his sorrel, patted and eased the nervous beast to the ground. Meantime David shifted against a thick pine for support, rifle ready. Plain to see was plentiful blood leaked and flowing on his buckskin. The lawman should not have felt pity but he did.

"We should be back-to-back," Thom offered.

The blond was distracted. "Why's that?"

"We can shoot through the trees as they ride up, cover each other."

David nodded at the common sense and Thomas crouched at the other side of the wide pine. By now the Indians, tall on their mounts, were galloping in a circle. When they charged, it would be from all directions. Whooping and hollering commenced. A brave shook his army-issue rifle in the air, others with rifles imitated him. The rest brandished bow and arrow. The leader reared his horse up upon its hind legs. For certain each rider in the party was ready to die if the fight called for it. The Indians' painted faces showed the fervor of holy men.

"Injuns can't shoot straight," David mumbled. Then the brave with the tall headdress kicked his mount and gave out a loud, chilling yell. The signal ordered a full attack at the trees and it commenced. The riders were like the spokes of a wheel, running hard from the rim to the hub. The whites gripped their guns.

Redskins got to the tree line in a galloping fury, some dismounted right off. They opened fire, as did Powell and McClure. Puffs of white smoke flew into the morning air and bits of bark and tree limb jumped as the first round of bullets and arrows entered the stand. An arrowhead stuck into the tree inches from Thom's head.

McClure fired his rifle in succession, knocking a brave off his mount at his arrival at the tree line. Mount bolted, scared. Another brave jumped off his pony in a way that reminded Thom of himself as a boy. The Indian was canny, crouched behind a smoke bush before the sheriff could get off a decent shot, but he shot anyway. Nearby, another brave dismounted, the sun at his back. He held a fine, feathered hatchet and rushed the two whites who didn't react until he was close enough to throw. Damn if it didn't cut through the cover and slice McClure's arm bloody. Now the same *Lakota* pulled a second hatchet from his waistband. He drew his arm back when Powell fired his carbine, stopping the brave's courageous run.

The Indian leader was on his horse at the edge of the stand, directing and encouraging the others. He gave a sharp pull on the horse's reins to steady the animal so he could fire his rifle. He let loose four or five shots and all struck nearby the whites, sending their heads down low for cover. This redskin could shoot straight. Same time other braves had dismounted and they let fly with bow and arrow. Shafts struck pines and brush. Lucky shot hit Thomas hard at the bottom of his left boot, ripping the heel off. Scared the hell out of him. Gun smoke among the trees thickened. Time was slowing like it does when death calls.

More arrows hit, this time with a surprise: The tips were on fire, covered in dried animal skin wet with lamp oil. Another arrow landed and another. When the shafts struck, wrappings broke apart, sending burning embers about. The thick, dry underbrush was soon crackling flames.

Thomas's tethered horse was up from the ground and stomping. The white men kept firing. The sheriff used his Paterson to hit a brave attempting to let loose another fire-arrow. Bow and arrow fell harmless to the ground. The stand was now a smoky, darkened ruin.

McClure got up off the ground with grimaced effort. "Don't fancy burning to death," he said. Powell did not fancy leaving the protection of trees. The blond was determined, all Thom could offer was "good luck."

The outlaw was stoic. "Always been lucky," he said and moved out.

Thomas came to his horse and un-tethered it, gave it a slap. It bolted toward the open plain. When he turned back there was a redskin not a yard away. The brave had a curved, long-bladed hatchet, he came down with it from high over his head. The lawman barely had the time to put his rifle up. The blade-edge cracked the Wesson in two, right at the wooden stock. It slide on down the wood and grazed Thom's arm from wrist to elbow, drawing blood. The brave had a knife in his other hand and thrust forward with it, but Thom had the Paterson drawn and fired. The unfortunate Indian was hit, sending him back into the brush for good.

*   *   *

At the same time, McClure emerged from smoldering trees. Smoke cleared. He was out in the open with three braves. One of them was the mounted leader with the headdress. The blond had discarded his rifle and held his trusted six-shooter in one hand and his knife in the other. Indians were taken aback by this wild-maned man, and hesitation cost them. McClure fired at the horseman. The leader was lurching about on his horse, hard to hit.

Get hit he did, once in the shoulder, which turned the redskin around and made him drop his rifle. The white man followed that with his Bowie and he stuck it from fifteen feet deep into the rider who fell from his horse with a thud that knocked his headdress off. McClure wheeled to the other two braves just as one let loose an arrow that struck him in the upper leg, just a whoosh then a thud as sharpened flint entered flesh. That brought hot burning about to split the limb. The force knocked the blond off his feet. That saved him. The second brave was shooting a rifle and missing. McClure rolled toward the oncoming redskin. He stopped and let loose the last shots in his pistol, hitting the Indian, putting him down.

David was reaching with purpose to his belt for bullets when he got stuck again. The shaft went deep into his back, piercing pain. The blow knocked him flat on his face and forced blood into his throat and out his mouth. He struggled to respond as the brave readied another shaft.

On the opposite side of the tree stand, Thom emerged onto the plain. His eyes were stinging, visibility nil. He was determined to join McClure for the rest of the fight.

A gust of wind blew smoke and sand aside. There appeared two braves not ten feet from him. One possessed a rifle and the other's bow was strung and ready. The two Indians had the drop on him.

Time slowed. Thomas pondered the occasions he figured his life would end any second. He was afeared the first time, second time too. But he came to learn how to face death with a cold heart.

Now the lawman knelt on one knee, turned sideways and let loose with his six-shooter. He emptied the weapon, using an open palm to cock and fire. Both adversaries were hit. It was right then he felt the arrow strike. Hit him hard in the chest, right where his heart was beating. He tumbled onto a tangle of thorn bushes.

The sky fell and covered him like a blanket from another world.

*   *   *

When Thomas came-to, he was on his back, the tree stand charred and smoldering. It was un-Godly quiet, save for the chirping of a solitary bird, calling with a long tweet, then another tweet. He looked into the air, didn't see the bird. He was not dead, he wondered why. He reached up, plumb scared, touching the top of his head. There was no blood, he had not been scalped.

Prickly thorns pulled at his skin and he used a hand to lift the snarl of branches and free himself. He crawled into the clearing. First thing he saw were two dead Indians laid out on the ground, rifle and bow clutched in stiff, pale hands. Thomas did not feel sorry for them, he was dying himself. He must be dying. He was shot deep in his heart with an arrow.

He strained to examine his body. He did not have an arrow shaft in him. He stared at a still and blue sky, saw a hawk swoop across his vision. He blinked and began the effort, taking his time, of standing up. There was no arrow in his chest. He glanced at a shaft on the ground nearby; that was the one stuck 'im. His own thoughts made no sense. He looked down at his vest, torn and ripped at the pocket. That's where he had been hit.

The jade statue was lying in the dust at his feet. Buddha was cracked in two nearly equal parts, clean as you please. The stone had caught the blow from the arrow. He picked up the green pieces and clutched them. He thought of his beloved. Emotion seized him, slow at first. He had to clear his head.

He found his pistol, reloaded, looked and listened, unaware if enemy remained. Had he and McClure killed the entire lot? He moved around the edge of pines to the other side where smoke was clearing.

There was McClure, face down in the dust, three feathered arrows stuck in. Next to him was a dead Indian with David's blade in his flesh. Nearby two more dead braves. A trembling, brown pony stood company to the sad tableau, head bobbing. Buzzards appeared in the sky, gliding easy. Scavengers have all the time in the world.

McClure was barely breathing. Thomas bent on a knee. Easy-like, respecting the shafts in his back, he turned his companion over, looked into the man's face. The blond's eyes opened. "What are you doing alive?" he whispered.

"Took some good fortune."

"How many arrows I take?"

The lawman did not want to answer that query. McClure looked peaceful enough.

"Three or four," Thom said.

"Hell, might as well get up."

The outlaw didn't budge. He reached out and took Thom's hand. "My mustang," he began, "in my saddle bags, greenbacks, you take 'em."

"Not mine to take."

"You turn it in and we know the men who'd get the money."

"What do I do with greenbacks?"

"I won't be damned so long if you do something good."

Now wordless. David's skin was pale, his body shook in short tremors. His eyes got the faraway look Thom had often seen.

"Smoky sky reminds me of Shiloh," the blond said.

"We were set in good, you kept coming."

"We took the sunken road. A lot of blood but. . . Did you see me?" McClure coughed dark red. His color got white, his eyes closed. The sheriff held his hand. Nothing else to be done.

Thomas looked around at the fallen *Lakota*, a tangle of dead. He noticed that one of the braves had a handful of cheroots in his waistband. What's an Indian doing with a white man's smoke? Senseless, the attack was baffling.

McClure died then. In the sky, damn buzzards glided closer.

VII

Made a sight. Powell ambling Topeka's Main Street on a bloodied sorrel with the covered body of outlaw David McClure laying across a trailing horse that bore Indian markings. Yelling youngsters and their barking dogs ran with him, and store owners' faces appeared in windows. By the time he made it to the Marshal's office, a peach-faced deputy was outside, taking his hat off, scratching his head. He stepped into the street and took the tether from the trailing horse and secured it as Thomas hopped off his mount. The young deputy was wearing an open coat the color of sand and it was flapping in a stiff wind.

"Sheriff, you alright?" the boy asked like he meant it.

"I am fine, thank you," Thom replied lying. He was hurting, blooded. He looked hard into the deputy's eyes. "Would you tend to the departed? He was an outlaw but deserves a burial. See after my mount, it's been through a lot."

Thomas did not wait for an answer, he was up the front steps. The boy nodded like he was used to taking orders from serious men. He led the sorrel and the pony off, even as he shooed away a gathering crowd of curious.

When Thomas got to the door, he could see the Marshal inside, looking out at him. Then the portal opened. Quinn's man, Jackson, greeted with a grunt. Thomas hobbled inside, seeing as the heel of his boot had been sheared off.

"Sheriff Powell," the Marshal exclaimed, as the tattered fighter before him made quite an impression. "What in Lord's name happened to you?"

Never talkative, Thom was quiet now. He nodded. "Marshal," was all he said.

"Who you have draped under that Injun blanket?" Quinn inquired.

"That would be David McClure."

"The dastardly gun for hire?" Topeka lawman spoke with pretend fear.

"Him."

"And where did he meet his end?"

"Up Nebraska way."

"Nothing there but Indians."

"It was Lakota did him in."

Jackson let out a weird yell which was unwelcomed. "You're a lucky man they didn't do *you* in, Lakota like to scalp," he offered.

The Marshal slapped Jackson on the back. "Common knowledge Powell is a fighter," he began, "those Indians are lucky him and McClure didn't kill 'em all."

"We did," Thom said with fists clenched. He made some picture, a warrior after battle. Quinn swaggered to a table and poured three brandies into glasses. "I know it's barely noon," he offered, "but I would say you could use a drink, medicinal purposes."

The words were the truest Thom had ever heard the Marshal utter. He took the proffered libation. Jackson toasted "To our blessed union," and threw his down straight off. Marshal Quinn sniffed his brandy as if that told him something, then he moved his hand in a circle, swirling the liquid before gulping. Finished, he offered up his glass to Thomas. "To the last ounce of bad blood," he said.

It was uncertain what that meant. It could have been a peace offering, which would have been joshing on Quinn's part. Thomas grasped the brandy and drank the three fingers in a slow gulp. Went down fine.

He took the glass and tossed it at Jackson, who caught it, nice catch. The deputy was perplexed. He held the vessel like he didn't know what to do with it. Finally he set it down on the table. The Marshal had a stern look set in.

"Left-hander," Powell stated.

*   *   *

He remained in town for a bath, a shave, and a meal. He checked into the Plymouth Hotel to sleep off the fight with the war party.

By and by Quinn brought a sawbones around. The sheriff had already doctored himself best he could, said he was fine though he was less than that. Truth be told, the Marshal's visit was not to check on Thom's health. Quinn was more interested in how McClure died. He asked if the outlaw spoke of his killing spree. He asked about his blood money. Thomas played it dumb, did the job convincingly. "We fought braves to the death, wasn't time for talk of things you ask about," he testified. Marshal seemed satisfied, hell, he seemed relieved.

Powell did not sleep proper that night. Powerful dreams grabbed and would not let go. Discomforting images of flashing gun barrels and spraying blood. The painted faces of the natives stared. Black and crimson birds swooped in the sky of his dreams. Even as he lay in bed, his body jumped in the presence of demons.

* * *

He departed Topeka, stopping by Boot Hill to make certain David was interred. The plot of land was a lonely spot down a sorry path overgrown with bramble. The sun was high in the sky. The lawman sat on his mount looking down at the wooden marker. "McClure, Outlaw," was scratched in.

Book Three
Jayhawk Justice

I

They were married on the first day of the New Year 1869. Weather was fine, an early thaw, blue sky was the deep shade of great bounty. The ceremony was held in a small church located at the edge of town, with the verdant woods beyond. It had a white clapboard bell tower, an ornate brass cross affixed at the highest point.

Baili chose the place. It was constructed of red bricks. She found brick most appealing, told Thom the finest love was brickwork. Thomas did not rightly appreciate such fancy. What he did appreciate was the way she considered herself and her life. The new land she came to was hard and unforgiving. She had her share of suffering and death, including that of her beloved father. Hardships were daily, she saw killing, more than a young'un should. All of that did not matter, she woke each morning like she believed in something, and was thus prepared for come-what-may.

Reverend Buttle presided over the sacred ceremony. The bride wore a dress of white silk and lace, the groom a gray suit with a lily flower pinned on the lapel. The man of God said words that neither Baili nor Thomas fully understood except those that spoke of the unbreakable bond that was being created between this man and this woman.

Finally the Reverend said "Now by the power of the law of the state of Kansas, and by witness of the Lord creator, I pronounce you man and wife." The married couple wore smiles to further warm the winter air.

*   *   *

Thomas had taken the halves of the stone Buddha that saved his life and fashioned necklaces. He and his bride wore them Wedding Day. The green jade caught light and sparkled. Slim and Red were at the ceremony, as were Ben DeCamp, Mary Dwighton,

Amos Maplewood, Dorothy Lysander, Doc Atley, Nathan Farnsworth and the Missus, Ned Tyrel - seemed most of Lawrence was either at the church or came by the town meeting hall on Massachusetts where the reception was held. In honesty there were folks did not care for this union. A white man and a yellow woman did not seem natural. But even doubters conceded the quality of the occasion. Thomas was a war hero, a lawman, and a man who treated everyone decently. Baili was smart as a whip and guileless as a mountain stream. Nothing under the Lord's sky could tarnish the day's beauty. Folks at the ceremony whooped and applauded when Mr. and Mrs. Powell kissed for the first time. Then one and all headed to Massachusetts Street where a fine fiddle band waited at the reception.

*　　*　　*

He resigned as sheriff shortly after that. He had served well for two years and it was understood that it was no job for a newly-married man. Instead, he bought himself a small farm off the road to Topeka.

Raised chickens and goats and got a dog. He and Baili kept a large garden on the side of the main house. They grew greens and onions, squash and potatoes. Had a corral with a half-dozen horses and plans to raise more. There was a living quarter for hired hands, though it was empty at first. It was Thom's intention to employ a good man or two, soon as he got up off his feet as a rancher.

He had a mind to hire Slim, who wasn't much use for other things, seeing as he had only one good arm and a hole in his foot that left him limping. 'Course a one-arm farm hand wasn't the most useful kind. Turned out loyalty won over business sense and Slim had himself a job.

For her part, Baili made the homestead a right comfortable place. She had an eye for the way things should be arranged, and in short order the house became a home. All kinds of goods were mail-ordered from San Francisco, including seeds for vegetables and fruit that came from China; different types of herbs and tea

172

that were both for enjoyment and for help with things that ailed you; kinds of dried fish arrived, one in particular called squid in English and in her language *yiu yu*. The creature was the strangest thing Thomas had ever seen, dried or alive. There were also joss sticks which were incense that Baili would light some evenings, making the house smell pleasantly.

This was a new world to him, a welcomed one. He embraced it lest it go anywhere. His unfolding life, youth, the war, being a lawman, brought him to her. In quiet moments he felt blessed and pondered on the dispenser of all blessings.

*   *   *

One day the past came calling. Baili returned inside from hanging wash on the back line. Thomas was at the oak table near the hearth. He had a telegram. She was not one to ask for information from her husband if none was offered, so she waited while he sat and read. When he put the message down, she crossed to the great iron kettle. She ladled soup into a wooden bowl and took it to her husband.

"This is good for you," she said. Thomas knew her ways, he smiled. "Telegram from Ben," he said. Baili sat. He wanted to tell her what was on his mind. He knew she wanted to know but would not ask. Steam rose from the bowl that was set between them.

"Connor Quinn was well acquainted with Chester Whitbread," Thom said.

"Mr. Whitbread was the man who hired. . ."

". . .the outlaw McClure."

"Did Quinn kill the Professor?" Baili had a right notion, though asking the question did not provide an answer.

"I cannot say, I know that the Marshal has been deceitful. There are public records of commerce, those two were in cahoots." Baili looked at him funny, not knowing the word cahoots. "Quinn and Whitbread had big plans for themselves," he clarified.

173

Baili listened earnestly. She spoke to the heart of the matter: "What can be done?"

Thomas considered a spell before he answered. "I can't abide Professor Hedley meeting the end he did, so surely undeserved. McClure is gone, he received just deserts. He was a hired gun, and a bad man, but did not hang the professor."

"You are not the law," she said with a tone that carried no judgment.

"I am not," he readily conceded.

"But still you want what is right," Baili stated. She spoke evenly. Her voice was familiar music that he had never heard before. She was not enamored of her husband's dance with danger, but she was with his stubborn sense of justice.

Thom reached out to the bowl of steaming broth and held it in both hands. Baili looked into his eyes like she was reading a book.

"You don't like the Marshal," she said. "There are not many people who make you feel that way."

"Something about the man, the way he flaunts his own life," Thom said. Then he waved a hand as if to dispel talk. The soup smelled good. He took the wooden spoon, drew a spoonful, and had a soothing taste. He drew another, blew on it, and held it for his wife who tasted.

Then he noticed she was holding her hands on her stomach in a particular way. She saw him staring. "Soon there will be smaller things," she offered happily. He did not comprehend until he saw the glow on her face.

*   *   *

It was spring time and it was a moonless night. Thomas could not sleep. There was no sense lying there listening to his own breathing. He got up nice and easy so as not to disturb his wife. He went to the front room, had a smoke. Sitting next to an open window he could smell flowers from the garden. Slim had helped him run the plough through the field to the creek across the way that marked the homestead. Now the odor of earth passed gently through the air and settled him.

He hadn't thought about the war in a spell. That was good, life goes on, but this night memories came. He sat and blew smoke from his pipe out the window. Wisps of white floated like ghosts. Why do some men perish? He had been in a dozen hard scrapes, men falling left and right; fiery bits of metal hurled through the battlefield, any number could have struck him ending his life or crippling him. He had been lucky, skillful, any way you look at it he had been spared. Was it for a purpose?

Thoughts came to Baili. He had done true when he cast aside folks' judgments and courted her. He pondered the way she slept, soundly. The look on her face in sleep was like she was with angels. Since her stomach had begun to grow she had become even more beautiful.

As he smoked, his thoughts continued their wandering. He thought about his dog. It was called Boxer on account of the man who gave it as a wedding gift said that was the type of dog it was, came from Germany. Boxer was gray and black, with a short stump of tail and sad looking eyes that nonetheless shone intelligence. It was a willing dog, and did a good job of watching the homestead, running around all day, following Baili, sniffing here and there, barking at everything what wasn't in its place, sometimes barking at the wind if it didn't blow right.

Boxer did have a certain, peculiar habit that Thom had come to expect. The animal barked late into the night. That dog gave a solitary yelling howl at the darkest hour. Thom had figured Boxer was calling out, heralding the coming dawn, though what could any master know of the goings-on in an animal's mind?

Finished with his pipe, he lowered the window. He checked his time piece and realized it was the dead of evening. Even now there was the faintest glint at the horizon. He listened for Boxer. That dog should be starting up. Thom waited, paced the front room, stretched. Too quiet; he got a feeling. He picked up his five-shooter and pulled his suspender straps up over his shoulders.

He ventured outside. Cloud-cover made the evening air foggy, creating poor conditions to see. There was a wooden crate out front that Boxer was partial to. This night the animal was not there. Thom made his way 'round back. A coyote howled in the foothills at the horizon. There was no reaction from Boxer to the wild animal's plaintive call.

Thomas had built a proper doghouse in the back yard. Boxer stayed there during the day, when he wasn't chasing critters away from crops, or roaming free in a wide pasture. Thom came upon the dog-house and it wasn't until he was close that he could see. Boxer lay in the doorway, quiet and still, dead. Its tongue was hanging out strange, bubbly foam spilt from its mouth.

Thom tucked his Paterson into his waistband and scratched his head. His first thoughts were that the animal just up and died. Perhaps it had eaten something it should not have, like a dead critter. Then the dreaded thought occurred it had been killed to silence it. Another coyote bayed in the cool night air. Stiff wind blew into the ex-lawman. It was like the passing of a bolt of lightning.

Thomas was seized by the sense of danger like a parent shakes a naughty child. He placed his hand on the pistol and turned to the house. Then the sickening sound of a blast from a shotgun shattered the peace of the evening and about shattered his soul.

The eruption came from inside the homestead. Thom broke into a full run. His mind got steely cold and quiet, reacting to peril. He knew Baili was where the gun went off. He cursed that he ever stopped being a soldier. He should not have become a husband and homesteader.

His burst onto the porch tore the screen door off the frame. The Paterson was out and cocked. Nothing existed except their bedroom, where she was. His life did not flash before his wide eyes. There was only the barrel of the gun.

The bedroom door was full open. He smelled a sharp odor, burned gunpowder. The wall was pitted and ruined from the discharge. A body on the floor, just inside the room. For cold, sick seconds he could not tell who it was.

Then he saw Baili. She was in her cotton nightgown holding a shotgun. On the floor at her feet was a man dressed in dark clothes. He was as full of bleeding holes as you could get in one blast. The now silent fellow gripped six-shooters in each hand. In the growing light, Thomas saw the pistols' pearl handles, recognizing them. Corpse was Jackson, Quinn's deputy, dead as Boxer.

Baili lowered the double-barreled weapon at the sight of her husband. She had a look in her teary eyes. It was not the countenance of fear but of defiance.

"I am real glad, Thomas," she said, "that you taught me how to use this."

II

Words can't bear the weight of emotion. Words failed to describe his rage. Jackson might have succeeded in his murderous intent if kind fate or sleeplessness had not taken Powell outside that night, if the howling of a coyote had not awakened Baili in time to hear unfamiliar footsteps in the hallway.

Thom was on a steady, trusted palomino riding west along the road to Topeka. Time didn't matter. Normally he might ride hard, this occasion he felt the need to take stock. The day had a clear sky and gusts that carried the scent of spruce. He could hear blackbirds calling to each other like winged creatures do. When he was a boy he made no note of such things. In war, the smell of flowers conjured battles fought in meadows. War made him acknowledge the powerful effect of nature on the way a man experiences his life.

It was Baili showed him the pleasure of simple joys. She liked strolling the quiet side streets of Lawrence, past people's houses. They would stop at a home and she would say she liked it, and shared with him why, might be the front porch's lattice work, might be a trellis full of white jasmine flowers. They would sit in finely crafted wicker rockers outside Dwighton House, doing nothing but bearing witness to the quiet night and the rhythmic sound of the chairs' runners. What fine peaceful memories.

Quiet moments now far away, nary a tender thought. Though a gentle breeze blew prairie lavender, he was oblivious, hard mood lay over him like the coarsest burlap. He was glad to have hard feelings for company.

*　　*　　*

As he rode the winding road, he pondered war's end. After the death of Quantrill, he was promoted to an officer. He was an unlikely candidate, couldn't read and write so well, but he had killed the leader of the bushwhackers. Aside from that, his prowess in myriad battles was military record. Thomas Powell, leader of men, deservedly became a Captain in the Kansan Third Regiment.

With that promotion, his contingent was part of three separate Union armies in Tennessee. Most of the state was secure, but Rebel remnants, commanded by a sad-looking General named John Bell Hood, kept up the fighting. Hood's army was driven from Georgia by Sherman, and what was left of it came into the mid-South looking for an easier fight.

Captain Powell and his company of veterans held the dug-in center outside the city of Franklin. One warm November afternoon in 1864 the Grays came in straggly waves, with more bravery than brains. Union officers had the men hold fire until it was nigh impossible to miss the ragged lines of assaulters. Thus lots of Grays got kilt.

What he witnessed at Franklin was war at its worst. When Confederates not already shot made it to twenty yards or so of the breastworks, Powell ordered his men to shoot into the air, thus avoiding further butchery. The Southerners staggered back the way they came.

Strange power, after three years of war, he lost his will to fight that day. Soon enough after that the rebellion was over, the South surrendered, a blessed event. He went home to Kansas.

*   *   *

He was at the junction where the road led to Main. He pulled the palomino back to come into town slow, and he placed his right palm on the handle of his pistol. Never did like Topeka.

It was Saturday. There were businessmen about, cowboys mixed in with citizens, and farmers rolling by in buckboards. There were finely dressed ladies, and children running with their barking dogs. He came upon the Marshal's office and there was the young deputy who greeted him months before. The boy doffed his hat.

"Sheriff Powell, is that you?"

"It is."

"Good day to you."

"Good day."

"You here on business?"

"I'm not a lawman anymore."

"Didn't know that."

"It's a fact."

"What brings you to Topeka?

"I want to talk to Quinn."

"Our Connor Quinn?" he stammered like there was more than one man by the name.

"That's right, son."

"Marshal's not here, Sir."

"Where would I find him?"

Young man hesitated, torn between duty and politeness. Thom admired that. Finally, the boy squinted and said, "At his place, ranch up in the foothills, off the road to Abilene." The deputy smiled, the boy had kind eyes. Thomas shook his hand, wished him well, hoping the Law would not corrupt one so earnest.

Thom and the Palomino found their way out of town and up the road in measured time. The fork that led to the Marshal's ranch was well traveled. At a distance there was smoke from the chimney that made the ranchhouse easy to spot.

Dark thoughts would not leave Powell's mind. Echo of a shotgun's blast, his family in harm's way. After a winding ride of miles, here was his destination. By this time he was real cold-eyed.

*　　*　　*

Connor Quinn was a man to be assured of goings-on around him. So it was no surprise when two long-eared gangly hound dogs had run out to meet Thomas as he arrived at the ranch. They barked, jumped, sniffed, and barked, first circling 'round then following the horse and rider.

The Irishman was on his front porch. It was a warm day and Quinn had just finished shaving; he was wiping his face with a cloth, pulling up his suspenders. Finished, he waved casually as Tom hopped off his mount.

"It's Thomas Powell."

"Marshal Quinn."

"What brings you to Three Forks?"

"Three forks, don't know what that is."

"Name of this place, my spread, got three roads converging into the valley. I been meaning to make a sign that says Three Forks!" He sounded rightly proud. The visitor did not respond, but rather tethered his mount and followed Quinn inside his place.

Straight away the story was confirmed that the Marshal of Topeka was a hunter of game. Folks who had something agin 'im opined that Quinn liked shooting things that could not shoot back. Gossip was true for inside the comfortable cabin of logs there were deer heads, bucks no less than ten point, mounted on the far wall. The great head of a moose was mounted on the varnished pine plank sidewall. In the middle of the floor laid a sizeable bear skin rug, complete with head and a fierce-enough-looking face full of teeth. On an oak table with a night lamp was set a big-ole stuffed raccoon with claws bared. Although Thomas had shot animals for food and hide, like most folks, he did not abide trophy hunters. Struck him as a cowardly way to act brave. He stepped 'round the furry floor covering, he would not disrespect the great bear.

"Let me offer you a drink." Quinn said.

"Water would be appreciated." So the Marshal ladled a mug full; he poured himself a whiskey, and invited his guest to sit at a rough-hewed table near the hearth. Both men drank their libations.

Marshal knew that as host he was obliged to speak first. "I can suppose why you're here. That nefarious fellow Jackson, may he rest in Hell."

Thom took a breath, not sure right off which words to say. "Bad blood aside, I take exception going after a man's family against the rules of God and men," he stated.

The Topeka lawman got a serious long-faced look, like the weight of the world was upon him. "It is a perplexing thing," he offered. Drumming his fingers on the table, he gazed into the hearth like it was a gypsy's crystal ball. "I don't rightly know," he began in slow cadence, "Jackson quit not one week before I heard what happened over your place. Don't have a clue why he would act in such a murderous manner. Very glad to hear you and the Missus are safe."

Any intended kindness fell on deaf ears. Thomas's jaw was set hard when he said, "He was your man."

Quinn acted surprised, "my man," he repeated like he never heard of the notion. "He was an employee of the great state of Kansas, as I am and as you were."

"He seemed more."

"What did seem like to you?" The Marshal got a twinkle in his eye that Thom figured was the whiskey.

"Watched your back, laughed at jokes. He was not his own man, he was yours."

"Then he departed the job, I heard nary a word, he skedaddled."

"You say."

"Well," Quinn played exasperated.

Thom stayed at it. "Why would a deputy become a killer in the night?" His voice had a tone. He was fast becoming annoyed at the drumming on the table. Quinn was a man unused to being addressed in such a manner. He finished his drink in a gulp. He stopped his finger-rolling and set his gaze.

"I don't care for the edge in your words," he stated.

Thomas sniffed. It had been a long ride from loving arms to this hostile place. "My tone is not the worst of it, Marshal."

Quinn got up from the table, poured himself another drink, two fingers. "How's the water, need a refill?" he inquired. He acted like he was pondering mightily as he settled back at his seat.

"You don't like me, I know." Quinn took a breath, let it out. "It's that old story, I did not serve in the foolish war," he said with a wave of his hand.

"I'm not here to argue about the war."

182

"We agree on that much."

"No sir, there were men not speaking English, just off a freighter back east, get lined up and sent into battle, they were told they would be fighting for their new country."

Quinn chuckled, though he was a cautious man and did not do it impolitely. "You sound like a politician, I can see you've given this thought. No, know what you sound like? a crusader," he corrected.

Thomas payed no mind to Quinn's words, he finished with what he wanted to say by adding, "What those poor men fought for was the right of another to buy his way out."

Quinn listened patiently enough, then he spoke. "You know what that is? I'll be most honest with you. That is their misfortune. War is a gathering of guns, neither victory nor honor. Sorry lot of men killing each other without a clue as to why. Therefore a man with smarts removes himself from such a situation."

Thomas told the truth as he saw it. "A man does not run from a fair fight, the war between the States was a fair fight."

Quinn got a tad agitated. "Get your facts straight, I did not run from a fight, I walked, and it was legal!" he said and laughed at his own poor joke. The Marshal's breath smelled of spirits. He looked hard at Powell, and spoke confidentially: "My former deputy, damn him, was on his own. You believed he hanged that professor, I can tell you that Jackson greatly resented the false accusation. I reckon he lost his mind and did something terrible, he always was touched in the head."

Thom was surprised some at the marshal's frankness. His mind ran over the things he knew and did not know about the matter at hand. Quinn slapped at the wooden table top and stood up. He went on over and took a cheroot from the mantle over his hearth, lit it up. The sight of the stogie made Thom think of the ones he spotted in the waistband of the dead leader of the Lakota war party.

Quinn waved smoke away from his face and spoke. "You know, I recall the show in my office when you tossed that glass. Left-hander, right-hander, I know it had to do with the hanged professor. It got me thinking so I asked that twit Muller. He in fact assured me he is not certain left hand right hand no hands, he told you what you wanted to hear."

Thomas stood up. He knew Quinn was smart. Now cards were on the table. "Marshal, the men McClure killed, and Hedley, were done in because of land-rights they had that someone wanted. Railroads gave the land and business as usual was expected. These men wanted something out of the ordinary, they proposed to help Indians."

Quinn, not a bad actor, seemed perplexed. "Help Indians? Well that is the craziest notion."

"It's what I believe."

"What else do you know?"

"I know that Whitbread had business with you."

"Wouldn't call it business, not in the successful sense. We had dealings."

"There is a bill of lading for a Winchester, purchased by you for the Boss, wound up being used on my deputies when McClure got sprung."

"Birthday gift as I recall, what the boss did with it I do not know. My part is neither a crime nor your concern and that's your last question Boy." No man likes being called Boy, strange but Thomas didn't take offense at the sharp words.

Quinn made a sound like an animal, harrumph. "Enough of this old, tired talk," he stated, "I'd like to show you something any fighting man can admire." He strode over to his far wall, where he had oak shelving. He gathered something lying in the shadows.

When he turned back to his guest, he held two weathered handguns. "Know what these are?" The pistols were flintlocks made of dark wood and cold metal. These weapons were from the war of independence waged by the States against the British Empire, nigh one hundred years ago.

"These belonged to my grandfather, also named Connor. Things of beauty, aren't they? Made in Germany, some place called Bavaria, you can believe that." Thomas could see in a glance the weapons were fine. Constructed with care and craftsmanship, seemingly in prime condition.

"They're good pistols," Thomas said politely and dismissively.

"These here aren't any old flintlocks, they are dueling pistols, perfectly balanced. Pistols like these were used by gentlemen to settle arguments that had gone too far to be settled by other means. My grandfather killed two men with these guns. My father killed one back in his day. For my own part, I have not yet had the opportunity."

Thom figured the Marshal was playing a game best not played. "I can't say I have interest in arranged shootings," he offered.

"Squabbles were different back then." Quinn's thick eyebrows rose as he held one of the guns up to the light. "Flintlock was in use three hundred years, until the ball and cap kilt folks better."

Where was the Marshal going with such talk? All Thom knew was that a man was holding a weapon, so he was alert.

"Simple and complicated is what these are," Quinn testified. "Piece of flint, piece of steel, and a place for the spark to touch gunpowder." He brought the weapon close to Thomas to demonstrate. He pointed a finger: "Here's the hammer, and the mainspring, this is called the frizzen and right here of course is the pan."

"I see."

"Powell, would you care to duel?" Quinn got a funny look, a whiskey-face, still it was hard to read. Thom understood: yeah the Marshal had avoided war, but he was no coward. The man was baiting, unafraid to die, happy to kill.

Thomas was an old hand with braggarts. "We shall not duel, those are impressive pistols I thank you for showing me," he said with finality, then added, "You know why I am here." Quinn shrugged and put the damn guns down. Took his time speaking Outside the window, crows were squawking in the yard. Quinn crossed over and banged on the glass with his knuckles, sending the crows off.

"I do know why you are here, to accuse me of outlaw activity, outlandish notion," he stated.

Thom saw no reason to pretend. "You know more than you tell."

Quinn laughed, he had to stop snorting to speak, an unpleasant thing. By now he had ceased pretending to be civil. "Who knows the answer to the puzzle, if indeed there is a puzzle to put together. It is a damn mystery, like the rest of this God forsaken life on the prairie."

With that the host moved to the front door and opened it. He turned to his guest to usher him out. "I'm not obliged to tell you a damn thing," he began, "Not about Jackson, nor Whitbread. And I'd like you to remember I have a badge and you no longer do. Do not get in my way son, I will uphold the law at your expense." Quinn got a look like he was much satisfied with his own words.

Thomas thought him a whiskey-fool. Worse, he had the urge to kill the man and end it. "Thanks for the water," he said. He started to leave the log cabin. The Marshal stopped him at the doorframe. "Powell, what comes next?" Thomas thought about it, he did not rightly know what would come next.

"Tomorrow," he said and stepped outside into the bright sun. The hound dogs were waiting at the foot of the steps.

*   *   *

Thom's mount was frisky riding to his homestead, the animal knew it was heading home, it did not mind being kept in a canter for a stretch. Evening air was cool, the moon bright in the sky. Arriving at the crossroad to Abilene, he slowed, then stopped. He listened to silence save for crickets. He removed his hat and ran a hand through his hair and gazed into the night. Abilene was a lost acquaintance, once well-known and now un-encountered for a good while. The town made him think of those days right after the war, when he came back to Kansas and did not know what to do with himself. His ma was gone, he had no family, and was haunted some by the war, like many fighting men. Seemed best to start something new, alone.

He hooked up with a fledgling ranch outside of town, he was hired to break horses. A likely job as he'd lived with the animals his entire life and knew the work of domestication. Nonetheless he did not take to the task, was no good at it. Horses were magnificent, wild, and full of unknowable fire. They commanded his respect and admiration. Weird but he was saddened seeing a horse's powerful kicks become a common trot and its fiery eyes extinguished.

So he did not last in Abilene. When he heard that the pitied town of Lawrence was rebuilding and seeking a sheriff, he decided to give that a try. He knew how to handle situations that were difficult and worse. The idea of keeping peace after a war was an appealing thing.

Blessed fate brought him to Lawrence, he would not have otherwise met Baili. He did not want to owe it to destiny. That means life is uncontrollable, try as you may. It means that a man's days are spent acting out what has already been written. That was a lamentable notion. Doesn't any man make his own future or at least have a mighty say in its creation?

There is a thing, Free Will, Christian folk speak of it. Thomas felt like it was an answer to destiny. If he possessed free will, he could craft his own life.

What to do with this formidable man, Quinn? What would a Christian do? Thom knew holy men existed, Jesus and Buddha, most likely there were others. They were all living men, how did they treat their mortal enemies? Did they forgive and forget, or did they do more when there was no other way?

III

Connor Quinn had nary a use for Nebraska. When he was a youngster he courted a girl from Lancaster in that territory. Her father owned the general store in town, thought himself a big man, and was not shy to testify that he despised Irish people. Called them potato-eating laggards and no-accounts to their faces, worse to their backs. Quinn was Irish by way of Kilkenny County, three generations removed. Girl acquiesced to father's wishes, and the young man was no longer courting. Connor pretended not to care, but he liked the girl and was truly hurt by the shameful slight.

Quinn was in business with a Nebraskan back in '60. Man was both dishonest and a drinker, thus making a poor partner. Furthermore, Nebraska was a wild land, with many more Indians than whites. The territory was a place where civilized people could not go about as they pleased.

It *did* have one redeeming quality. In the western part of the state the Platte River split into the north and south branches, the former snaking into Wyoming, and the later flowing down to Colorado. In that far area a man with a rifle, a will, and a level of savvy could find Big Horn Elk, a smart game animal that made an outstanding trophy. So the marshal would, now and again, forget his deeply held contempt for Nebraska and venture from Kansas into the cow-town state. It was a long haul to get through the wild land, but he had a spot back home on his cabin's wall just right for a trophy. He had not yet bagged an elusive elk but he remained hopeful.

This particular day, a cold one in late springtime, he rode with three others. One was the brand-new mayor of Topeka, the honorable Bunsen W. Fogarty. Not a bad fellow he was, with a round countenance, short legs, and an even temperament. Was a fine mayor if a mayor best served the people by respecting all railroading interests. He did that very thing and thus Fogarty's job was secure. This made him friendly, a good listener, always at the ready for a laugh. He could not, however, shoot a gun worth a lick, nor did he see particularly well, and had never hit a rabbit much less a buck deer, much less the prized Big Horn.

Also cantering the road through Republican County was Myander Bushmill, a railroad man. He was a tall, dark, secretive sort, who wore gold rings on his pinky fingers. It was said he was from back east and had powerful friends among the iron-horse crowd. Rumor told he started out a Pinkerton detective, a particularly rough-edged one. Some said he later worked for Wells Fargo as a security agent, and his reputation for seriousness grew. Then he settled in with the Union Pacific Railroad in what the boys who ran things called a management position. In short, the man had done well for himself if money and position were the measure.

On this hunting trip, Mr. Bushmill carried a brand new Wesson repeater rifle with a military scope. It was a fine and expensive weapon, shipped to him special from New York. He and Quinn had just been recently acquainted; the marshal looked sideways when he was told how much was paid for the high-powered rifle.

"That's some greenbacks," the lawman said, "Can you shoot it worth a darn?" At this point men might mention their service in the war, whether on the winning or losing side. Battles fought in, firearms discharged. After all, if you survived combat you shot passably. Real railroad men could well be shooters, but as a rule didn't fight in the war, any fool knew that.

"We'll find out about my prowess," Myander intoned. He laughed hardily like moneyed people do. He had a cigar stuck in his mouth that he was quick to tell came from Cuba, exotic locale, though his listeners had barely heard of the place. All three men tried a Cuban, not a bad smoke, but Quinn would, as the party approached its destination, tell all to put the smoking things out. Wild elk can sniff tobacco a mile away as an unnatural odor.

It was a fierce day, weather-wise. Wind was calm but the sky was filling with dark, moving clouds. In the distance, it appeared worse weather was heading in. Fine with Quinn, elements didn't matter to the hunt. "Elk move in bad weather," he said.

He was dressed in a buffalo skin coat and a coonskin cap such that with his great size he seemed larger than the horse he was riding on. The animal beneath him snorted like it would rather be anywhere else but on a trek with such a load.

Bushmill began talking about a place called Africa, which lay across the great eastern ocean. There, according to the railsman, were all description of wild animals. The entire continent was a hunter's paradise. He spoke of creatures called bull elephants, big as stagecoaches. He spoke of lions and tigers, wild cats that like the raw meat of men. Bushmill went on about how rich men back east are fond of venturing to Africa for big game hunting. They call it *Safari* and it is a grand time.

Quinn was a common man at heart, not one to travel far afield, but nonetheless he was interested in talk of Africa. Big game hunting, yes. He might go there himself one day, see what he could bag. Then Bushmill said it was black men's land, many more of them than whites. Imagine that. Marshal was disinclined to cross an ocean to be among those he deemed inferior. Thus ended talk of the Dark Continent.

*   *   *

A fourth man on the hunting trip was a skinny youngster name of Josh. He wore a beige riding coat and was introduced by Quinn to the others as a new deputy. Youngster wore no badge. What he did have were two colt revolvers, one holstered, the other tucked in his belt. Not fit guns for game hunting, and the way he rode last in the group, one hand on the reins, his eyes darting, made him look like a young gun along for personal protection, which he was.

That night they camped in thick woodland, after bagging rabbits and wild pig on the approach. The air was cold, the plain's wind had picked up considerably. They grouped around a great fire of dried cedar and pine. They ate and told stories. The boy sat off from the three older men. Above, the moon was hidden behind a white shroud that hung broadly in the darkening sky.

Quinn had taken off his oversized coverings and was drinking Scotch whiskey from a tin cup. The Mayor of Topeka was smoking a nicely crafted wooden pipe. He had made a long-winded point of telling that it was fashioned from *teak*. "Hardest wood known to be," he claimed. Bushmill must have been hungry because he had already eaten an entire rabbit and was now poking at an undersized pig.

The Marshal got up from the campsite, stretched his arms out and made a sound like the roar of a bear. Then he waved at the dark. "Wasn't far from where we entered Nebraska," he began, "on the other side of the river, back in, when was it? 1858, I'd say. I was in the employ of the Northern Kansas Railroad. Took the first rides on the laid rails. Me and others rode on a flatbed car, out in the open, shooting buffalo. You never saw anything like it, great herd, a thundering mass of animals making noise with their hooves that could be heard over the banging engine, clanking wheels and our own fire power. I personally shot two hundred and ten head on that trip."

The Mayor let out a puff of smoke from his teak pipe. "Two hundred buffalo?" he echoed.

"And ten. As I recall the entire railroad party killed up to a thousand during the ride over and back."

"Why that is unbelievable," Fogarty offered.

"You can believe it," Quinn added. "Killing buffalo was the business of railroads back in the day."

The mayor, happy being a part of campfire talk, called out to young Josh. "You see son, buffalo meat fed the rail workers." The young gun managed a polite smile.

Marshal snorted. "That and the fact that there were too damn many of them and dead buffalo are no use to redskins," he added in a tone that dismissed what Fogarty had offered.

Bushmill stopped eating and took a drink. He sniffed at the air, considered the marshal. "I was on a buffalo killing trip nigh ten years before that date, when the first partial rails came through the high country. I'll tell you, herds back then measured ten miles long and two miles wide," he said, proud to have such information. Mayor whistled, and the boy Josh spit a stream of tobacco juice.

"Don't see herds like that anymore," Quinn said.

"Which is a good sign indeed," Bushmill added. Fogarty threw in an "Amen."

Moments passed in silence save for the sounds of the night and the fire. The marshal stood up and leaned into the group. He spoke in a humble way, as if to take them into his confidence. "Gentlemen, we are seeing the end of buffalo, then the end of Indians, such a momentous occasion." He got quiet, and the others didn't know what to make of his words. Then the lawman unfixed his trousers and peed into thicket.

"Here's to buffaloes and Indians."

*   *   *

Next day when the hunting party reached the north fork of the river, they took it. They crossed the water by way of rocky shallows. On the other side was a long, level plain. In the distance were visible green woods and foothills rolling to a range of snow-capped mountains. The valleys of that range led through Nebraska to Wyoming Territory, untamed country. The Marshal turned up the collar of his furry coat and exhaled a lungful of steamed breath.

Sun was high in the sky and a stiff breeze blew into them, which was good for the hunt. There would likely be elk in the woods ahead and the wind would help hide the smell of men until it was too late for the quarry. Quinn was riding up front swaying slow, back and forth in the saddle, while underneath him his horse struggled with the weight. He was humming to himself some song or another. Momentarily, he broke into a whistle. The man had the bearing of a carefree soul who thought the world of himself and the land he lorded over.

Mayor Fogarty was behind him, holding the reins of his palomino with one hand while he bit on jerky with the other. Bushmill rode alongside, tall in the saddle, holding his shiny Wesson across his chest. The glass in the scope of the rifle flashed in sunlight. Tagging along a polite distance from the three was the gun Josh. The boy stared into the flat distance and the looming mountains ahead, pretending there was something to be on the lookout for.

Marshal had just removed his coon hat, ran a free hand over his head, and looked up into the sun, thus warming his face. He returned the hat, then gazed up at a lone, brown hawk, swooping and gliding in graceful arches. Quinn was thinking there must be a critter about. The hawk was steering down for a kill. Law of man and nature - the strong take the weak.

Then. Just then there was a sound, Crack, in the distance. Connor Quinn lowered his gaze to the tree line ahead as the sound echoed in the air. The others looked. What *was* that? It came from the woods where the group was heading. Strange, appeared it might be the discharge of a gun, but who on God's earth would shoot and for what purpose?

Answer came with a thud that hit Quinn with such force that it knocked him straight backwards off his horse and hard to the ground. Animal bucked and jumped, as if greatly relieved. Then it bolted and galloped away.

The Marshal was on the ground, with a hole in his head now bleeding crimson red. The entry wound was small, a deceiving thing. On the other side was an exit wound large as a gold dollar. Shot had been fired from the tree line, good quarter mile. Hell of a shot, hell of a shot indeed.

Josh reacted best he could, pulled the Colt from his belt, gave his horse a kick, and moved to the head of the group, like he could help and protect. Mayor let out a sound, started choking on his beef, wound up spitting it out, and managed to dismount, fact was he *fell* off his horse. Bushmill, quicker to act, used the sight of his gun aiming to see something in the woods ahead. But his was a nervous animal, the horse was shimmying this way and that, so he accomplished nil.

All three spooked men were now off their mounts. They moved to Quinn, who was dead as can be, shot midst forehead.

His eyes were big and fixed open, there was a snarling look on his face and his tongue hung out his mouth. The way he was dressed, in that buffalo coat all pulled up around him, made him look like a game animal, bagged by a hunter. Some trophy.

IV

It was perplexing. It could not be rightly determined what happened to the celebrated Marshal of Topeka, except what was obvious, he had been killed.

That day on the flat land, Josh rode into the woods from where the lethal shot had come to have a look see. He was young and foolish enough to spoil for a fight but he found none. He made his way around the dense trees and underbrush, searching for a campsite, some indication of a shooting stand. There was nothing and that is what he reported back to the other men. Bushmill, a hard case, was not convinced, so he went off and had a look-see. He came back shaking his head, no trace. Whoever shot Connor Quinn was gone with nary a clue as to how and why.

Fogarty and Bushmill determined it best to forget Big Horn Elk. The Marshal's horse had bolted and was gone, damn the animal. It was decided to chop pine into logs and lash them Indian style for dragging the victim back to civilization. That was some endeavor, hauling a body the size of Quinn's through land such as they came from. Josh did the dirty work, it was his mount that did the dragging. Good thing both the boy and his horse were young and strong, the task was backbreaking. Fogarty and Bushmill forged ahead, swapping stories as they ambled, happy keeping polite distance from a dead man. Of course they were sorry for the Marshal, and as civilized men would demonstrate respect. As far as personal feelings, neither knew Quinn well. Fact was, the newly departed was not a man to enjoy warm remembrances.

Once back in town, word spread faster than that bullet traveled over the short-grass fields into Quinn's brain. Newspaper had a curious headline: "Beloved Marshal Victim of Lord Knows What."

In days that followed, a federal officer arrived by rails from St. Louis to investigate the tragic occurrence. Dressed in a twenty-dollar suit and a derby hat, he had a twinkle in his eyes that left everyone thinking dandy for sure.

'Course the Railroad got involved. Quinn, a true friend of the Iron Horse, had earned their sending famed Pinkertons. Those were a rough group, veterans of the winning side of the war. They asked sharp questions and pushed folks around. They milled about stores and banks and cat-houses, all in the name of doing their job regarding the Marshal's untimely end.

So Topeka was a hot bed. Officials and folks running this way and that investigating. It was mostly righteous indignation that powered the thing. How could a man get kilt in such a nefarious way was the question.

*   *   *

After all was said and done, there were more ideas about what happened than facts to go by. One of the Pinkertons posited that the marshal's death was an accident, a random gunshot fired by unaware hunters on the other side of the flat plain. Lord, a fellow would have to be unlucky to get killed like that, born under a bad sign he'd have to be. It was like shooting into the air and having the bullet come back down with deadly results. In addition, that part of Nebraska was scarcely travelled so odds were against two parties in search of game. All concluded that posit was farfetched.

Another Pinkerton opined that the killer was an Indian, one who finally learned to shoot straight. Idea was some buck or another coming upon the hunting party. Maybe the brave or braves tracked them and took the opportunity to kill a white. The word assassination was used, like to evoke the martyred President. Real unlikely, but still there were folks willing to buy that. Problem was it ran against the natives' notion of honor. Red men believed that if you had to kill a man you do it up close. They were not likely bushwhackers. Besides, there was nary a trace of any campsite or shooting place out there in the woods, white or red.

A state investigator offered the James Gang as the villainous assassins. That line of thought was popular, made the newspaper. Idea there being that Jesse got tired of being chased and turned the tables. Passable notion, 'cept that outlaws weren't in general rifle marksmen. When word arrived that the gang robbed a train in Missoura, hundreds of miles away, this notion knew no credence.

It was the derby-wearing gent who offered the craziest notion: David McClure done the deed. That the blond was a crack shot was widely known, that boy had a reputation. Veterans of the war came forward in the investigation to claim that hell yes Quick Shot could hit a man from a quarter mile away. That made folks wonder if McClure and Quinn had something personal between them and that the latter's death was about settling some score.

But McClure was dead and buried, wasn't he? Well, turned out the undertaker back in Topeka was in such a hurry to get the outlaw in the ground and get paid the pittance he had coming that he had the corpse in the earth *pronto*. Then, a harsh period of rain followed in town, causing a mudslide at boot hill, washing away the simple grave marker that had been set. As a result, no one knew for sure where he was buried, so it would be nigh impossible to exhume the pine box.

'Course, this last theory would have required nefarious involvement from Thomas Powell. The man was beyond such reproach to all but enemies, so the theory had few adherents.

At the end of the three-ring circus that was the official investigation, the suited types from the railroads, the slick-haired ones from St. Lou, and the common folks who sat on barstools drinking ale could only offer whatnots and maybes.

Time went by, like it does. Investigators went home, and the state of Kansas got itself a new marshal.

*   *   *

Thomas returned to his homestead. His beloved was truly glad to have him back. While he was away Baili had attended with great care to their business at the ranch, even got them a new dog. Now with her husband's return, the homestead was as it should be.

Her stomach was larger, she glowed more beautifully than ever. When they lay holding each other, he would close his eyes and allow a contented smile. Such blessings were humbling and were to be treasured.

One day after his return, Baili found her husband out back, in a sweat chopping wood. She had with her a telegram, sent by Ben DeCamp in St. Joe. It stated that he was heading west for the newspaper, he would be stopping by the ranch.

As it happened, he arrived on the 4th of July, 1869. Baili sat near the hearth at a table of birch. Portal had a view of green hills, it was a nice spot for cutting and mixing vegetables she had grown and the herbs that came mail-ordered from California. There was a wonderful aroma of potato leek soup rising from the iron kettle. Just outside the men sat on the back porch, having a smoke. Both were in pine rockers made by Red as a wedding gift. The chairs were functional enough, if creaky.

Ben had a rolled-up copy of the Missouri Star. "Heard about Marshal Quinn, I imagine," he said casually.

Thomas did not react much. "Was the talk of the town for a good spell," he replied.

"Big news in the territories. That's a bad end, getting shot dead on a hunting trip by some person unknown. Regardless, it was a most skilled shot."

Thom put tobacco in his pipe but did not light up. Instead he held a matchstick in his fingers and looked at it. "I'll tell the truth," he started, "I was not bothered by the news." His face reddened, he turned away. "Should not have said that," he offered.

"No sense being polite, Captain, I met the man."

"Not Christian to speak ill of the dead."

"Well, far as Quinn being a Christian, let the Lord make the call."

The men shared a coarse laugh, like they had during war when making light of dying meant survival. Thom got up from his rocker and looked out over his land. He spoke in slow cadence. "I have spent precious time pondering the men who pull strings and the men who get pulled. But what's done is done, our lives are now. Every new day I think less on my time as sheriff."

Ben had an encouraging air. "Good for you Thomas. The Marshal and Jackson should go straight to hell: Good riddance."

Thom knew his friend pronounced those harsh words for his benefit, like the dead men were not worth talk. It was a sound notion and accepted: "So what else is new in St. Joseph?" he inquired to change the topic.

DeCamp took the newspaper, used it to wave at a buzzing bug. "Just the usual local affairs, coarse gossip." Then the reporter tapped at the paper with a finger. "One item of interest though."

Thom stayed where he was. "Better tell me about it, Ben," he said. "I'm working at reading well but you go ahead." The guest cleared his throat and adjusted his spectacles.

"Well, headline here says 'School and Orphanage to Open.' Some kind soul donated greenbacks to provide shelter for Indian children who have lost their parents or who are half-white and thus unwanted. They'll get an education, learn English."

"That a fact?"

"Over in Hiawatha."

Hiawatha, Kansas, in Brown County, was a small community half a day's ride from Lawrence. Founded some dozen years earlier, it was named after an Indian character in a literary work, though few folks knew that.

Thomas took the newspaper and read, pointing with a finger, he was in fact a passable reader. "I don't suppose the feds or railroad money paid for this orphanage," he offered.

"Suppose not."

"Private donation, it says."

"From a person or persons unknown, what they call anonymous."

Just then Baili came outside with two glasses of home-brew ale, a most welcomed libation to celebrate the holiday of the 4th. Ben thanked her kindly, as the husband and wife exchanged a look that any fool could see was love. She went back inside to resume her cooking. The men rocked and sipped.

"You're a lucky man, Captain."

"I know that I am."

"And she's a lucky woman."

"I hope so my friend."

Ben could see that Thom was contemplative, didn't seem right for such a day. He leaned forward and slapped his old commander on the knee. "What can we toast? Let's drink to something."

Thomas gave it thought. "Jayhawk justice," he offered and the men raised their glasses.

V

He fell into a sleep, dreaming of a child, his son. The boy had a wild head of curly hair, the sort he remembered his mother having. Child's skin was a golden hue, the babe's almond-shaped eyes were the color of a summer sky. Those eyes gazed at the world calmly, sure of the existence of goodness, peaceful in the knowledge that every new day was a chance worth taking.

THE END

ABOUT THE AUTHOR

Matt Cutugno is the author of three novels and eleven plays that have been produced in New York, Los Angeles and across the country. He has been a frequent contributor to *Stay Thirsty Magazine* for the past six years. He is from New York and currently lives in California.

THE GODLESS MEN

Made in the USA
San Bernardino, CA
27 July 2019